Voices From the Mausoleum Presents:

# Sincerely, Departed

## An Epistolary Zombie Horror Anthology

Copyright © 2024 by Voices From the Mausoleum

All rights reserved.

No part of this publication may be reproduced, distributed, or transmitted in any form or by any means, including photocopying, recording, or other electronic or mechanical methods, without the prior written permission of the publisher, except as permitted by U.S. copyright law.

The story, all names, characters, and incidents portrayed in this production are fictitious. No identification with actual persons (living or deceased), places, buildings, and products is intended or should be inferred.

Book Cover by Grim Poppy Designs

Curated by Angel Krause from Voices From the Mausoleum and Cat Voleur.

Interior Formatting by Cat Voleur

# Contents

| | |
|---|---|
| Introduction | 1 |
| BEING A BETTER HUMAN<br>Angel Krause | 3 |
| THE NAME OF THE STAR WAS WORMWOOD<br>Tom Coombe | 21 |
| PROJECT LAZARUS<br>Casey Masterson | 31 |
| ZOMBIE FREE RADIO<br>Sophie Ingley | 51 |
| LEFT ON READ<br>Samantha Arthurs | 61 |
| LEAK<br>Maria Hossain | 79 |
| TR1X13<br>Andrew Harrowell | 89 |
| DEAD IN THE WATER<br>S.C. Fisher | 99 |
| Fullpage image | 112 |

| | |
|---|---|
| FODDER<br>Emma Jamieson | 113 |
| GREGORY GWINN AND THE BLIGHTHAND KNIGHTS<br>T.T. Madden | 122 |
| WHEN IT'S DONE<br>Andy Rau | 129 |
| WASTE NOT, WANT NOT<br>Madeline White | 149 |
| SPLINTERS<br>Christina Wilder | 158 |
| #4LIFE<br>Patrick Tumblety | 169 |
| WET PAPER OVER SHARP BONE<br>Cat Voleur | 199 |

*This book is dedicated to all the humans and infected alike who sacrificed their lives so we could write these stories*

# Introduction

Dear Readers,

First and foremost, thank you.

You could be reading anything right now and you chose this insanely niche indie horror anthology, for which I am sincerely grateful. (Even if you skip past this introduction, I'm just glad you have the book.)

I myself am very wary of introductions. It's a terrible thing to pick a book based on nothing but a cover or a recommendation, get it home, and have too much revealed right before starting. I can promise you now, this isn't going to be one of those introductions.

I asked Angel if she would let me write this because I just feel so passionately about what we've created together. Like with everything else along the way, she was extremely amenable to it. She doesn't know that I'm about to gush about how brilliant she is, and how lucky I was to be the one with her working on this.

She could invite me to just about anything, and I'd say yes, because I trust her creative vision and know that the working experience is going to be a blast. But I struggle to think of anything she could have invited me to that I care more about than epistolary zombie fiction. These are probably the two subgenres that have meant the most to me over the years, the two I keep coming back to over and over.

Most people don't know this, because it remains unpublished and terrible, but the first book I ever wrote was an epistolary zombie novel called Untitled.docx. It was written as the virtual diary of a teenage girl trying to make useful observations about the outbreak to give to the rescuers she and her friends *hope* are coming. My first published story, *Sole Survivor*, was about zombies. My debut book, *Revenge Arc*, is all true-to-source epistolary horror. And now, thanks to Angel, I get to have my name on this absolute beauty of an anthology, which is everything I love about both of these subgenres.

I'm so glad that we seem to be living in a resurgence of epistolary appreciation. Horror is rooted in the writing of diaries and letters and logs—just take a look at Bram Stoker's *Dracula*. I love that we're starting to see that presentation evolve to include more modern means of communication. I hope that we can do something to bring the same level of respect and consideration to zombies, which are still tragically snubbed by the mainstream and indie reader communities alike.

Angel and I spoke a lot about what sort of stories we hoped to receive when we opened the call, and what our aspirations were for the collection. It was important to both of us to showcase why zombie fiction isn't just a silly, throw-away genre. It is in our exploration of the undead that we find elements of characters who are the most human—for better and worse.

Looking back as far as George Romero's *Night of the Living Dead,* this is a subgenre that has always been about social horror. It plays off of survival, loss, isolation, the unknown, and our own worst instincts. It is one of the most relatable types of horror fiction, despite somehow also being some of the most speculative and largest in scope.

That is the core of what we wanted to share with you, reading this. Through letters and emails, text messages and chatlogs: zombies are not to be overlooked.

Thank you, reader, for seeing the truth in that.

Sincerely,
Cat Voleur

# BEING A BETTER HUMAN

## Angel Krause

*Dear Marie,*

*Inside this box you'll find a few things regarding my work at the Outpost. I'm sorry I couldn't deliver this myself, but James is a trusted friend from the world before this one and I knew I could trust him to get it to you safely. I know batteries and technology are hard to come by where you are, so I transcribed my audio logs.*

*I hope the words will inspire you and maybe in some way make amends for our separation and what I've done. All that is left to do in a world run by monsters, is to be a human. Be the best human you know how to be.*

*I love you with all my heart.*

*— Mom*

## Day 1 of Being a Better Human

Day one of me trying to become something in this world that I couldn't in the previous. I decided maybe this could be a way to clear my conscience. To go on record, some shitty torn up papers I found in this abandoned building, so that if anyone ever finds my body they won't think I'm a total fuck up.

But I am. Mostly.

I don't know what day it is. Once withdrawal kicked in, I lost track of everything; including my own sanity. I know that I've been on my own for a long time. If I had to guess? Maybe six months? Maybe a little longer?

At the first sign of shit getting bad, I wasn't in this crumbling bank on 8th street. When this got bad, and I mean really fucking bad, I was visiting a friend in the hospital. ~~Not really a friend.~~ A friend from school had gotten really badly injured on campus and so I went to see her. To make sure she was okay.

Honestly, I was more than a little under the influence when I went. ~~Guilt~~ So the events are a bit hazy.

I remember not being able to go into the room.

I remember sitting anxiously in a chair in the hallway.

I remember the screaming starting from somewhere else in the building.

I remember the running and the panic.

I remember clutching onto doctors and nurses as they flew by me. Hoping someone would give me a goddamn answer.

Then my survival instincts, or whatever was left of any, kicked in and I ran. I didn't know what I was running from or where I was going to run to. I just ran. I collided with a patient who was out walking with their IV bag, and we both fell to the flood. We had slipped on something and after looking over both of us I realized it was blood.

"Nasty bitch," I said to the woman who had been walking. I blamed her for the blood on my jeans and my name brand sneakers. How dare she run into me? What the fuck was wrong with her?

Day 1 of Being a Better Human

Nope. That isn't who I want to be anymore. So I'm starting over my count of being a better human. Day 1 until I get it right.

I should have felt bad for her. I should have felt SOMETHING HUMAN. Something kind. Instead I had felt repulsion. Now I just feel sad.

If I had felt kinder, if I was kinder, I might have tried to save that woman. Instead, as she reached out to me, I left her there. By this point the screaming was maddening. Chaos existed only in the sound in the halls. The echo made everything worse.

I remember people running into the stairwells.

I remember thinking what idiots they were.

I remember going straight for the elevator.

When it opened, that was when I saw one for the first time. It must have made it on with people trying to get away. There were two bodies on the floor of the elevator, and then the one that should have been dead but wasn't.

Once the doors opened, it turned towards me. I didn't get to look at it for very long before it was launching at me. The smell of its breath was putrid and as I tried to grip its shoulders, I found hunks of flesh and tissue missing. Snapping at me and trying to get to me, I rolled it off of me and ran into the elevator just as the door closed.

My back and palms were against the elevator wall and I couldn't catch my breath. At least I knew now why everyone was running.

Day 2 of Being a Better Human

I ran out of space on the scraps. It can be risky doing downstairs to the main level of the bank, but I did. I wanted to see if there was any water left in the break room. You can tell by the rooms that it was ransacked when infection started. People came in here for the money. They didn't care about the supplies. So when I locked myself inside, it was just for me. For now.

I wouldn't have thought this type of situation would be so cliché . I never heard how it started. Too focused on me, as usual. The hospital was just a really bad place to be at the time. I managed to get out using that elevator but the lobby was utter chaos. The sounds of teeth on flesh and screams is something that haunts me still. Adrenaline kicked in, but my brain just wanted me to find someone to help.

An adult. A professional. Someone with a gun? The security team had their hands full and as I could have guessed, they were utterly useless. One of them had already turned into a monster and was chewing on the throat of another. I got out of the building purely because of how many people were running around trying to get away from the infected.

Right, so I found a notebook when I went to get water and it even had a neat little pocket for my shreds from before. A collection of nonsense from the one bitch in the world who should already be dead.

Day 3 of Being a Better Human

I guess the next thing to be open about was my physical state once I found the bank. There is one of those things locked in an office downstairs, but otherwise there was no one here. Pure luck. Good for me. I had led a bad life but I didn't deserve to die or to be bitten. This was a-

Day 1 of Being a Better Human

So anyways, the next obstacle to overcome was withdrawal. I had a bit of a powder problem, just like all of my friends who lived in that neighborhood. Our real problem was the adults in our life not paying attention. I know, poor us right? Mom and Dad made so much money they couldn't be around. We still got all the things we could ever want. It was hard no matter how you looked at it. We just pretended it wasn't.

The first time I ever did coke was with my mom, actually. She was hosting an adult party on New Year's Eve when I turned sixteen. She was insanely drunk and figured what a great way to ring in the new year. Mother-daughter bonding.

It turned into a habit quick. I'll spare you the boring lulls of the fantasy of drug use. It wasn't a fantasy. It fucking sucked. I hated my life and I hated myself. It just quieted it down a little bit. But each time lasted a shorter time frame and then it reached extremely toxic levels.

The first day of withdrawal wasn't that bad. I know it started because the need was starting to make me foggy. Headache. I felt a general weakness. By the end of the day I was vomiting and convulsing. I was freezing, but I couldn't stop sweating. I don't remember much from those days. I know it took a while. Maybe about a week, if I'm guessing based on the puzzle pieces in my memory. The really fucked up thing, I remember was walking to the roof and almost jumping from the ledge.

If I'm honest, I don't know why I haven't yet. What am I even doing? This is such a fucking waste of time.

Day 1 of Being a Better Human

I'm running out of supplies. I'm down to two bottles of water and a granola bar. The power to the building finally went off. I always wondered how that worked. In the movies it is right away. No power and no cell service. I dropped my phone at the hospital so I have been dealing without it for a long time. It'll be winter in a few months and not having heat is going to be an issue. So I'm going to try and find some things to get me through. I guess I'm really writing this to hype myself into going.

Day 2 of Being a Better Human

My little trip took me hours.

I'm breathless. I managed to get into a general store near me and they had a lot of things I needed. But then I was trapped. I've been so disconnected from the world I didn't know these things had changed. Evolved? Mutated? Both?

There was one by the entrance and it was crawling on the ground with its feet and hands. Sluggish at first, but then spurts of energy would cause it to shoot forward at an alarming speed. The eyes were gouged out, leaving dark bloody sockets of nothing. I don't know. I don't fucking know.

It was smelling the air and reaching out. It seemed almost, pitiful? I stopped pushing my cart of items and I was looking around to find something to use as a weapon. I had never killed one or even attempted to attack one. My life in the post apocalypse was just as sheltered as the one before. I leaned forward to look around and the tires on my cart squeaked loudly in the silence. In a rush of motion, the monster was on top of a check out aisle and looking at me with its gorey, goopy holes. It smelled again and at least now it was away from the door?

I bolted. Shoving the cart into full motion and trying to get to the door. I was close. So close. I shoved the cart through the door and felt the outside air hit my face before my entire body was thrown backwards. I abandoned my cart and fell back to the ground as the creature scampered towards me. I've never felt fear like this. I'm pretty sure I

Anyway, it was terrifying. I could smell death on it. Drool and blood slipped down from its opened mouth as it pinned me. It was hesitating and I didn't know why. I wiggled against the bony fingers that dug into my shoulders. I lifted my knee up and forced it upward, hard, and managed to scramble out from under the infected.

As I stood to run, I noticed how lanky and frail it looked. It squeaked at me with no language but it was a high pitch sound I had not heard before. I slid against mystery liquids on the ground and made it through the door. It was right on my heels. By the time my hands touched the rail of the cart again, I felt a searing hot sensation in my ankle.

It had followed me outside.

It caught up to me too quickly.

It had locked its teeth around my ankle.

Panic ensued.

I began to kick and thrash to get it off, but it just wouldn't let go. The noise was causing too much attention and I could see several stragglers starting to notice me. This was not how I wanted this to go, clearly. The only thing I had close enough was the camping heater I had grabbed. I picked up the square box and slammed it down on the head of the once human gnawing on my leg. I lifted and slammed it down a dozen times before it caused enough damage to break free.

By this point, there were at least six other 'not humans' around me. I couldn't do it though. I couldn't leave all that I had collected. I tossed the smashed, bloody box into the cart and shoved it forward. Racing as fast as I could away from the others. They weren't as fast as the one that had gotten to me. I made it back to the bank, by the skin of my teeth. As I closed and locked the doors, the slower ones eventually showed up. They banged and banged. Their moaning loud given the stress of the situation.

"Fuck off!" I yelled at them, and then I laughed. How useless. I brought all of my supplies back up to the big office I've been hunkered down in. It wasn't enough for forever, but it would have to do for now. I barely made it out of there with any of it. I didn't get anything to treat my wound but I found a pretty unused first aid in the downstairs coffee area. It had enough to clean up the wound and bandage it. I didn't know what this meant, but I had a feeling it probably wasn't good.

I've heard the stories before they became reality. If this spreads the way it does in fiction, I'm absolutely fucked. So all I have to do now is wait.

Day 3 of Being a Better Human

I have a fever, that much I can tell. I feel sick to my stomach and my ankle is killing me. The wound itself hasn't gotten much worse, but I did clean it up again and use the last of the ointment to rebandage.

I did an inventory of my items to distract myself from the pain. My cart consists of the following:

X battery powered heater

X a case of water

X flashlight (one that winds up)

X sleeping bag

X several boxes of snack options

X various canned foods.

I had made away like a bandit and all I can think about is how I might still die anyway.

At least here, if I turn into one of those things, I won't be able to hurt anyone. ~~Not like I hurt Chelsea.~~

Day 4 of Being a ~~Better Human~~ Better Zombie

I don't know if I'm turning, but I feel better. The sleeping bag is so much more comfortable than my jacket I've been using as a pillow. I feel better rested, but I kept having nightmares. I think my close call at the store has really brought up a lot of things.

The point of this was to show I could change my mindset. When shit hit the fan, I really didn't like who I was. I'm still in high school. Was. I was still in high school. Now I'm completely on my own. I was a little more capable than I would have originally thought that's for damn sure.

But if I'm going to be better, I have to cope with this guilt. I should be honest. Chelsea is probably dead. Her family and anyone else that loved her is likely in the same position as those not humans that are still banging on the door downstairs. Fucking relentless.

Chelsea and I were not friends. When my mom and I moved here Chelsea wasn't someone I wanted to know. She was a target. An easy one. So I used her to show I wasn't someone to fuck with. I took all my rage and anger out on this girl that had nothing to do with it.

Day 5 of Being a Better Human

I had to take a break from that trip down memory lane. I guess I'm not going to be a zombie? My wound is looking better, but I don't have much to keep it clean if I want to be careful with my water usage.

I thought writing these things down was going to make me feel better, but I don't think it's working. The noise outside is louder now. I don't know if there are more of those things or what, but it is loud. I feel it echoing in my head in a way I can't even describe. It is like I can feel where they all are. I'm going to the roof tomorrow to test something out. For now, I'm going to take some headache meds from the first aid cabinet and try to sleep.

Day 5.5 of Being a Better Human

The sleep didn't help. The noise is just too loud.

I'm on the roof now, sitting with my legs over the side of the building. The air is starting to change. Fall, or whatever piece of that we get in the south, is starting. I can see, even though it is practically night, that trees are changing. The wind around me feels good, my skin feels hot all the time now. I don't think I'm running an actual fever though.

So when I said I can feel them? I mean it. I can close my eyes and pinpoint where they are. Without looking. Isn't that wild? What the fuck does that mean?

I can see flashing lights floating up and coming in my direction. Maybe a drone? Either way, I'm going back to my room. I don't trust anyone knowing I'm here.

Day 6 of Being a Better Human

I don't know where to start.

I know it is eating me alive.

~~It is my fault.~~

~~I killed Chelsea.~~

~~It is all my fault.~~

~~I don't deserve to live.~~

Chelsea is my fault. I'm the one who put her in the hospital. It wasn't supposed to happen like that. She was supposed to just land in the fountain and get wet. It was supposed to be humiliating and instead she-

It could have been avoided. If she had just left things as they were. She didn't need to involve adults. Don't people know that only makes things worse? I had a reputation to keep up. I had to show her that she wasn't going to be able to get in my way. That **NO ONE** gets in my way.

Day 1 of Being a Better Human

I hate what I did to her. When I think about how many times I made her cry. Or how many times I embarrassed her, I hate myself. More and more. I don't deserve to be here. I don't deserve to be alive.

She hit her head so hard on the side of the fountain. The corner where the stone center piece cracked her head. There was so much blood. Someone walking by screamed.

I can hear screams outside. They don't sound like human screams. They sound like those things. Screaming out to me and reminding me of what I did. The horror of my reality as a human being.

I don't deserve to be here.

I don't deserve to be alive.

Day 2 of Being a Better Human

I'm going outside today. I'm going to leave this notebook on a table near the entrance. If anyone finds it, they'll see my notes. They'll know the truth of how I am.

My name is Alison Merks. I am responsible for the death of Chelsea Sawyer and I don't deserve to be alive.

*[Street Camera 7,314]*

*A girl emerges from First Bank on 8th. She slowly walks out and looks around. Infected notice her immediately. Two move from the side of the building and start shuffling towards her. She stands still.*

*The first one to get to her goes down. She jumps in surprise. The second falls over as well. Something appears to be sprayed out on her clothing.*

*Five uniformed men come into view. She's shot in the arm and goes down. They collect her body and disappear as quickly as they came.*

### *Transcribed Audio Log of Dr. Francis Cobin - Tape labeled 14285*

**Dr. Francis Cobin:** Subject 17-19 years of age. Female. Biracial. Healthy.

I've lost track of the Jane Does, but this subject left a notebook with her name. Alison.

She was found at First Bank on 8th and has a wound reaching approximately 4.25 inches wide on her right ankle. The depth is to the bone and somehow healing has already begun. New tissue is growing and infection to the wound is low.

Her numbers are off the charts. She is clearly infected with the virus the government called C68-UD. She has no symptoms.

*(pause)*

The other subjects, people, haven't come with names and information. Just bodies with wounds to tend and a brain to monitor. After almost a year of doing this work, this is the first time in that time I've ever stopped to think about it like that.

I checked the numbers yesterday, and we are at 200,886 immunities. She makes 200,887. None of them have ever healed their wounds.

I've seen what they do to the subjects that are defined as immune. I've watched them take away my patients and turn them into monsters. The government here has no interest in helping anything. They are but a child playing with ants and a magnifying glass. Everything will burn if they don't turn themselves around.

---

### *Transcribed Audio Log of Dr. Francis Cobin - Tape labeled 14286*

**Dr. Francis Cobin:** Alison hasn't been allowed to be awake yet. She's been here three days prior to ending up on my table and no one will let her wake up.

I've been reading through her journal she left, the notebook left at the bank. This girl has been through a lot and I can't imagine how she'd feel knowing she had spent that time trying to be better only to end up here.

I keep pushing off the officials. They want reports and updates. They want to know when they can take her. I can feel the hopelessness of this endeavor, but I have to hold off letting them whisk her away to their torture chambers. I feel responsible for her now. I don't know how else to help.

---

*Transcribed Audio Log of Dr. Francis Cobin - Tape labeled 14287*

**Dr. Francis Cobin:** Alison favors my daughter, Marie. I keep having flashes of her when I look down at the table. Marie is safe, at an outpost, but I miss her so much.

What would she think of me if she saw this work I was doing? Her mom the hero? I doubt it. She'd be so disappointed. I'm not making anyone proud, myself included. One of the soldier types came in today. I don't know his rank, I hear muffled noises when they speak.

He got too close to Alison and I had to ask him to leave. His comments regarding her young body were more than unsettling. When I asked him to leave he tried to argue but I stood my ground. My hand was pressed into his shoulder, and I had enough of my own training I could easily dislocate it. He was nobody pretending to be somebody. He was rather enjoying being able to take advantage of the state of things.

I have to save her. For myself. For Marie. For Alison.

---

*Transcribed Audio Log of Dr. Francis Cobin - Tape labeled 14288*

**Dr. Francis Cobin:** Her notes read that she can feel the infected. As though she might have a connection to communicate in some way. I was unable to keep this to myself, so she will not be in my care much longer. The soldier types will take her and experiment on her using people with far less morality than I.

Marie, if this makes it to you, I hope you know I hate all that I've aided in. I have to do right, starting now and I can't be a part of it. They'll never let either of us just leave this place. Our only chance at peace is to die on our own terms. I know what I have to do. It will cost me my life but know I at least saved one person from true torment.

I love you so much, Marie. Don't trust the military. Don't trust anyone with power. I hope you're safe and that you know I tried to make it right in the end. Alison deserves so much more than what this fate would lead her to.

She wanted redemption. Instead they'll give her pain.

*(pause)*

Hell.

*(pause)*

No one deserves that. I guess today is my day one of being a better human.

*Recording ends.*

## *Medical Office*
## *Exam Room 122*
## *[Camera 7]*

*Dr. Cobin can be seen putting a solution in a syringe. She approaches the subject on the table and injects the solution into the subject's arm. The body of the subject convulses and shakes on the table. Dr. Cobin can be seen brushing the subject's hair before all goes still. Dr. Cobin is seen reaching down and gripping the subject's hand, using her free hand to wipe her face as though she were in tears. She exits the room.*

# THE NAME OF THE STAR WAS WORMWOOD

## Tom Coombe

**From:** Cheryl Colangelo <CherylColangelo1965@jumpmail.com>
**To:** Brian Colangelo <BColangelo@GreatLakesTech.com>
**Subject:** Checking in
*May 5, 2025 at 9:43 p.m.*

**Brian, if you get this message, don't come home.**

**Your dad and I wanted to call you last night with news about our diagnosis, but the cellular networks must be overloaded. I'm sorry you had to learn about this via email. (Assuming the home test kits are accurate. We're afraid to go to the doctor.) We know it's horrible news, but please don't come home.**

Honestly, I'm not sure how you'd even get home from Ohio. The army just shut down the interstates, placing concrete construction barriers and parking lot tire spikes near the exit ramps on Interstate 78 and Route 22. They've shut down the airports and stopped the trains in and out of Philly and Harrisburg. Even buses are off-limits. The Army uses them as makeshift ambulances, transporting new cases to the field hospital they set up in the Walmart parking lot outside Bethlehem.

I drove by the other day, my last day of work before the schools closed. The fear in the eyes of the people getting off those buses, soldiers barking orders, the families huddling together and being pulled apart...Brian, it was like something you'd see in footage from World War II.

I prayed the rosary for them when I got home, just like I pray it for you.

Your dad wanted to get out using back roads, but there are hunters – fisherman, I guess they call themselves – watching the countryside now and we know they'd want to examine our teeth. They've blocked off some of the roads, downing trees to make bottlenecks that force people to their checkpoints.

Their patrols have become more frequent. Gleaming, beefed-up Dodge Rams and Ford F-150s creep past the house at night, with six or seven men in the cargo bed, armed with shotguns and fire axes. Some of them wear ski masks but others we know, like Jerry Schiavone from the township supervisors and Dr. Mullins, who did your sister's braces.

"They can't be everywhere, Cheryl," your dad likes to say, but they really only have to be lucky one time, and that's it for us.

So we're staying put for now, keeping our heads down and staying indoors, waiting for news of some kind of treatment. I am praying that you'll do the same.

Love,

Mom

---

**From:** Cheryl Colangelo <CherylColangelo1965@jumpmail.com>
**To:** Brian Colangelo <BColangelo@GreatLakesTech.com>
**Subject:** "school" in session
*May 7, 2025 at 4:02 p.m.*

Brian,

Just writing to let you know we're still here, still OK, all things considered. We hope you have a good supply of bottled water. I know some people say boiling your tap water makes it safe, but there's still no official word from the CDC.

We saw our first "school" yesterday at dusk, thirty or forty of them shuffling past the house, pale and wall-eyed and shrieking the same phrase they all say in high parroty voices: "The ocean is coming. The ocean is coming," over and over.

"They don't have much time," your dad said. "Once they're in that chanting stage, they only have a couple of days to get to the sea."

(Don't worry. We're not there yet.)

They looked so ragged, I wanted to bring them food, water, clean socks...anything, but I know better than to approach them when they've gotten to that point. I've seen the video of that couple from Indiana.

Write when you can. You are in my prayers, as always.

Love,

Mom

**From:** Cheryl Colangelo <CherylColangelo1965@jumpmail.com>
**To:** Brian Colangelo <BColangelo@GreatLakesTech.com>
**Subject:** more news
*May 8, 2025 at 11:53 a.m.*

Brian,

I know you're probably worried about our food supply, but don't be. Your dad went on a buying spree before the COVID lockdown and we've barely made a dent in any of that food. We have enough canned soup and chili to feed half the town. We keep that quiet. It's not a good idea to let people know about your supply situation these days, even though the neighborhood is emptying out. We got some more bad news last night. Your old Little League coach Mr. Keppner is dead. He shut himself inside his garage last night and started his car after the webbing began to grow between his fingers. (He'd told your dad the virus was a hoax when this all started.)

I think about all the times he would finish mowing his lawn, head to the side of his house and drink straight from the hose, what seemed like a gallon at a time. I ask myself "Is that when it happened?"

I wonder the same thing about myself. I rarely drink from the faucet. It was one time, one tiny (microscopic, ha-ha) mistake last week. If I had switched on MSNBC five minutes earlier, I would have caught the same clip everyone on earth has seen, the president saying "...we now know it is not airborne, but waterborne."

You know your mom, Brian. I can't swallow pills without water and I had one of my headaches that day, and I'd left my bottle downstairs so I went to the bathroom sink and THE OCEAN BENEATH THE OCEAN WILL RISE AGAIN.

Your dad drinks his regular eight glasses from the tap every day. He says it tastes fine and it's not like he can get infected twice.

We try to hold onto our sense of humor as we pray for a cure. And for you, always.

---

**From:** Cheryl Colangelo <CherylColangelo1965@jumpmail.com>
**To:** Brian Colangelo <BColangelo@GreatLakesTech.com>
**Subject:** Still here, still safe
*May 10, 2025 at 1:29 p.m.*

Brian,

I know the incident here in town with the fishermen made the national news, but we're OK. No need to come home. From what I can tell on Facebook, that man had been selling bottled water for $300 a case.

The Millers across the street must have had an infection. Someone spray painted MERMAID VIRUS SICKOS INFECT THEIR OWN in black along their garage door.

(That's just a myth, by the way. I would never do that to you).

I admit that things are scary, but I'm trying to stay positive. Your dad and I are exercising more, walking the path along the Lehigh River three or four times a week, always at dawn before anyone is around. Internet has been spotty so we've stopped staring at our phones all evening, which means we're both sleeping better. Your nana never slept more than THE OCEAN IS COMING than four hours a night after she turned 60 and I'm glad I haven't inherited that from her.

Write when you can. You're in my prayers, as always. But please, don't come home.

Love,

Mom

**From:** Cheryl Colangelo <CherylColangelo1965@jumpmail.com>
**To:** Brian Colangelo <BColangelo@GreatLakesTech.com>
**Subject:** thinking of you
*May 11, 2025 at 4:44 p.m.*

Brian,

Sorry if I'm flooding (no pun intended) you with emails lately, but I saw something on the news about the "super school" that passed through Cleveland on its way to Lake Erie. Their skin was green, which apparently means they have the "freshwater" strain of the virus. The footage looked like it was near your neighborhood so I wanted to make sure you're OK.

Things are the same here. We attended mass via Zoom today. Father Berger talked about the great flood, and God's covenant with humanity. I admit I yawned a few times, but that's only because I had my first bad night's sleep in weeks. I blame the dream I had.

I was crouched on a slimy rock at the edge of the Atlantic, clutching a sea bass the size of a cat. The scales scraped my tongue and throat as I gnawed at the fish, honey, and my teeth were little needles, sharper and longer than the ones I'm growing. There weren't any signs or landmarks, but I knew I was in Massachusetts, but centuries before it became a state, or a colony, or even before anyone had ever uttered the word "Massachusetts."

Gusts of wind slammed the shore, ripping leaves from the trees but I still held tight, talons pressed into the rock as I gobbled down the fish. Other things that looked like me crawled down to the shore, their skin the color of spackle. We crouched on the mossy stone and waited, our faces to the sea. The waves, taller than anything you surfed when we went to Hawaii, rose and fell 10 times, 100 times, and then a fin the size of a cathedral broke the surface of the water.

We threw our heads back and in unison let out a long, low croak that burned my lungs, but that singing brought such joy. Oh, sweetie, I knew THIS was my God and someday I will follow the river to the sea to meet Him. He waits for me to descend to the Secret Ocean, the True Ocean. There we will all join His eternal host and swim like children between the teeth of His great pincers as the seas swallow the land.

I woke up to your dad sitting up in bed, looking at me.

"How tall would you say that fin was?" he asked.

I know how all of this sounds but really, I don't want you to worry, Brian. We're fine. The Ocean is coming the Ocean is coming so let me close by telling you that I love you and your dad loves you and we hope you're keeping safe and the Ocean is coming the Ocean beneath the Ocean will rise again.

You were such a sweet baby, our sweet boy our sweet baby boy such a sweet sweet boy and The Ocean is coming The Ocean will rise again The Ocean is coming and we will all swim in it so Brian my sweet boy please come home the Ocean is coming will rise again please come home come home come home sweet baby boy sweet boy the Ocean is coming please come home come home come home sweet boy baby the Ocean beneath the Ocean will come again sweet boy baby boy boy come home my boy the Ocean is coming the ocean is coming the ocean

**From:** Brian Colangelo <BrianCol79@jumpmail.com>
**To:** Cheryl Colangelo <CherylColangelo1965@jumpmail.com>
**Subject:** new email/visit plans
*May 9, 2025 at 1:57 p.m.*


Mom,


I'm sorry I haven't been in touch sooner. I tried calling earlier but the cellular networks are overloaded these days. I just wanted to make sure you had my new email. Obviously, with everything going on, Great Lakes Tech is cutting back and I was furloughed last week until further notice. I was thinking this would be a good time to visit. It will take awhile, since I'll need to take back roads all the way, but I should be there in a couple of days.


Love,


Brian

# PROJECT LAZARUS

## Casey Masterson

*Abstract*

Scientists across the United States have been in a race against time amidst the outbreak of the *lazarian virus*. This particular disease affects only the recently deceased, unless the living are harmed by the infected. Recent studies have found that the *lazarian virus* revitalizes particular cells in the brain, namely the cerebellum, the hindbrain, and the medulla. We hypothesize that restimulation of the frontal cortex will return humanity to the infected and, most notably, help to cure death itself.

*Transcript from the KBEL News Broadcast on 10.27.25*

**Heather Mitsuki:** We apologize for this interruption to your regularly scheduled programming for an important update. The infected have breached a stronghold in New

Jersey's Pine Barrens. I'm told we have footage of the invasion, but I have been advised to warn of its graphic nature. Viewer discretion is advised.

**The Video:** *The camera's lens was speckled in voids that rained red, blurry droplets. The visibility was helped very little by the camera's trembling. Two dark walls boxed in the voyeur with the lip of a desk overhead. Zooming in the video made the scene clear, cutting out the interruption of the rolling chair's legs. Something from above dripped onto the camera, causing another red tear to fall down the screen. The sounds were those of screaming and pleading were interrupted often by the snap of breaking bones and the wet tearing of skin. The carnage was limited to a sea of red until a woman fell into frame. She pushed herself up on her palms like a seal before clawing her way through the crimson muck. Her right foot snapped into a 90-degree angle.*

*Two new feet shuffled into view. The infected could be seen from the waist down. One of its hands was missing three fingers. The same arm had a trench carved into it with the serrated blades of teeth. Her bone shined in the ditch.*

*The prone woman screamed once the infected stepped a foot on her back. She spun, knocking her attacker off balance for a moment as she tried to shimmy backward. She waved her arms and kicked her good leg in a pitiful attempt to save herself.*

*That was when she made eye-contact with the camera.*

*"OhmyGod," she pleaded. "Help me. Please do something, please please—" Her speech turned into feral howls as the infected caught her flopping arm like salmon from the river. The woman was pushed downward. The predator pounced.*

*It had been a woman in life. Its long hair was now either matted to its head with blood or torn out in sizable chunks. Its mouth bloomed into its right cheek through a ragged hole. This very same cavern was used to create its twin in the infected's neck. Screams and protests were replaced by gurgling.*

*As the infected ate, its dead eyes locked on the camera, but made no notion of recognition.*

### *Transcript from the Recordings of Doctor Lawrence Baker*

**Baker:** We've all lost someone to this. Perhaps that is why the board passed over the only solution to this madness. I—We—should have known our research would stir the emotional ignorance of our patrons. They're content to wallow in despair and hopelessness. At the risk of repeating myself, we should have expected such a reaction. People react to stressful situations in astoundingly narrow-minded ways.

Without approval from the board, I will need to take matters into my own hands. Not just for the sake of our experiment, but for humanity. Consider this a journal, of sorts, to keep my thoughts organized. A traditional journal would simply be lost in my mire of notes and calculations. With this, at least, I shall know where to find it. Furthermore, if some injury were to befall me, it will make it easier for [Doctor] Jeffrey [Ahmbridge] to follow my thought process and continue our work.

Now, onto business. I am to meet with Adrian Lancaster on behalf of myself and Jeffrey. With luck, they will see the potential in our hypothesis and grant us permission to perform our experiment at their compound.

This is humanity's ember of a hope. It is essential for them to fan the flames.

---

### *Transcript from the KBEL News Broadcast on 09.19.25*

**Heather Mitsuki:** Thank you for tuning in tonight. I'm Heather Mitsuki.

**Darrel Rutherford:** And I'm Darrel Rutherford. Tonight's top story is the continued barrage of the Lancaster Corp on Atlantic County. Live on the scene is our field correspondent, Jessica Hayes. How're things looking out there, Jess?

**Jessica Hayes:** Pretty rough, Darrel. To recap for those of you who've been affected by the rolling blackouts and reduced cable coverage, Adrian Lancaster, a veteran and former police officer, has formed his own militia. They have taken over a research lab in the swamps just outside of Hayfield. Police are currently attempting to ambush the place in retaliation to the Lancaster Corp's recent raid on local businesses and homes for supplies.

**Darrel Rutherford:** And how is the siege on the compound going?

**Jessica Hayes:** Not well. Lancaster's militia seems to have access to heavier artillery than the police. If that wasn't bad enough, the noise seems to be drawing the infected to the area.

**Heather Mitsuki:** That sounds scary. Are you in a safe spot, Jess?

**Jessica Hayes:** Yes, I'm in the 'copter. Unless the infected gain the ability to fly, I'll be a-okay up here.

**Heather Mitsuki & Darrel Rutherford:** *laughter*

**Heather Mitsuki:** Well, thank you so much for that report. We'll be sure to check in later to see if the police have made any progress. Now, for our next story; Is the CDC getting closer to finding a cure? More on that after a word from our sponsors.

---

### An Excerpt from the Journal of Doctor Jeffrey Ahmbridge

LAWRENCE HAD THE LANCASTER CORP KIDNAP US. WELL, THAT ISN'T ENTIRELY ACCURATE. LAWRENCE HAD THE ADVANTAGE OF KNOWING THIS WOULD HAPPEN IN ADVANCE.

I HAVE NO IDEA WHEN I'LL BE ABLE TO GO BACK HOME TO SEE THOMAS AND MICHAEL. I'LL TRY TO KEEP AS ACCURATE A RECORD OF WHAT IS GOING ON AS I CAN TO KEEP THOMAS INFORMED IN THE AFTERMATH OF LAWRENCE'S STUNT.

I FELT SOMEONE JOSTLE MY ARM AS I LAY FAST ASLEEP NEXT TO MY HUSBAND. MICHAEL HAS A TENDENCY TO WANDER INTO OUR ROOM AFTER A BAD DREAM, SO I BLEARILY OPENED MY EYES IN PREPARATION TO PULL HIM INTO BED WITH US. INSTEAD,

I was greeted with the insectoid stare of night vision goggles.

"Dr. Ahmbridge?" The voice came from further in the room. I was too startled by the stranger's appearance at my side to do anything but nod. Unfortunately, that was enough to bring them to action. The intruder closest to me hauled me out of bed while the other appeared from the shadows, placing a sack over my head. I should have known these Lancaster Corp goons would be devoid of imagination, stealing their methods from dystopian media.

I heard Thomas begin to rustle in the sheets before he spoke. "What're you—"

"Go back to bed, Mr. Ahmbridge. Your husband will be safe with the LC."

Thomas followed us to the door. He pelted the Lancaster grunts with bewilderedly irate questions. They never spoke. His pleading inquiries were then turned to me, but they were softer, more concerned. "Jeff? What's happening? Did Lawrence really go through with it?"

I had only mentioned the desperate scheme of my scientific partner to Thomas once. My reaction to our research proposal's denial was to try a different

ANGLE. HIS WAS TO REACH OUT TO A MILITARISTIC COMMUNE. YOU CAN SEE WHY I DIDN'T TAKE HIS RAMBLINGS IN EARNEST, AND YET, HERE WE ARE. "I DON'T—" IT WAS AT THAT POINT I WAS SHOVED INTO A VAN, RUDELY CUTTING OFF ANY CORRESPONDENCE BETWEEN MY HUSBAND AND I.

"AH, JEFFREY, THERE YOU ARE," LAWRENCE BEGAN. I WOULD ONLY LATER DISCOVER HE WAS SIMILARLY CLOTHED IN A CLOTH MASK. "WE SHOULD GO OVER OUR NOTES AS WE GO OUT TO LANCASTER'S."

"FUCK YOU."

---

*Transcript from the Recordings of Doctor Lawrence Baker*

**Baker:** Jeffrey's moody disposition did not alter until we were provided with a specimen. In another situation, I may have understood his reservations about Lancaster. I'm not overly fond of the man's methods either, but sacrifices are needed in the name of progress.

Jeffrey and I have come too far, with too important a mission to refuse any opportunity we get. When this hellscape is over, when we conquer the *lazarian virus*, and even death itself, we will have time to shun those of lesser moral virtue.

Not before.

I did not ask Lancaster's militiamen how they captured our test subject. This was partially pragmatic, as any mention of casualties in the pursuit of science would have certainly soured Jeffrey to our cause even more. And yet, it was sedated, and brought into a glass enclosure at the center of our circular laboratory. A metal mask covered its mouth and it was restrained. The mask was also connected to various tubes that we could administer gaseous sedatives through.

Any bickering between Jeffrey and I silenced as the gurney was wheeled in. There was a physical shift in the air upon its arrival: one of danger, one of potential.

This will be our glory.

---

*An Excerpt from the Journal of Doctor Jeffrey Ahmbridge*

This is madness. Lancaster and his henchmen wheeled in our patient on a gurney. Even if we are to cure her, I have no idea how she is expected to live. She will be in agony. There is a hole where her right breast once was with broken ribs stabbing upwards. It oozes blood constantly. She has no right eye. Her left hand dangles by a thread, and her right foot is turned at an unnatural angle. Most damning is the hole in her head. Her temple has eroded into a canyon. Her skull shows spider-webbed cracks where skin was torn away, and her brain is visible in some places.

This is no way for anyone to live.

And yet, if we can find her a cure, perhaps she can finally rest at peace. Perhaps we can put them all at

PEACE TO MAKE THE WORLD SAFE (RELATIVELY, ANYWAYS) FOR ALL OF US.

FOR THOMAS.

FOR MY SWEET BOY, MIKEY.

FOR HUMANITY.

---

### Official LC Progress Report by Doctor Lawrence Baker

Day 1: The procedure is complete. Expect the test subject to respond within a day or so with our two-pronged treatment. This consists of the following: cellular and electrical manipulation.

Daughter cells are introduced to the brain, replacing the inactive with a biological circuit to send electrical pulses into the frontal cortex. Repeated electrical stimuli will be continuously administered until the brain regains its ability to synapse on its own.

At Doctor Ahmbridge's provocation, the test subject also underwent minor surgery to remedy the more damning wounds. Life support will be administered until necessary equipment can be acquired to mend the more substantial injuries.

Will continue to monitor.

Day 2: The test subject has yet to show any signs of progress. It only growls.

Will continue to monitor.

Day 3: An attempt was made to speed up the electricity's influence on the test subject. I will take full responsibility for the rashness of my actions, as Doctor Ahmbridge had no consideration in the matter.

The idea was that an increase of voltage to the circuit would speed up the process. The subject's skin was instead subjected to third degree burns and no change in cognitive status.

Will continue to monitor.

Day 6: Subject is now cognizant. Will collect and upload biological data and report back.

---

### *An Excerpt from the Journal of Doctor Jeffrey Ahmbridge*

The first thing she did was scream. I hope I never hear anything like it again, but, as we need to take care of her, I'm afraid there isn't a choice. She should be dead due to her injuries, yet she is being forced to live in the name of research. The screams are panicked, dripping with agony. It's the uncanny cry of the reaper being denied his due.

Lawrence was oblivious. He raced over from our monitors as my movement was still chilled by the sudden noise. Whether he noticed my absence, I do not know. He flitted about her like a bee in a garden; in an unorganized path from head to foot, side to side. All held nectar for him.

She wept from her eyes, from her wounds. As I finally made my approach, I could see her lips moving in between the wails of the banshee. At first, I attributed it to the tremors people can have in a fit of hysterics, emotion causing the mouth to chatter with the cold of emotional distress. It was only when I joined Lawrence at her side that I heard the unused croak of her voice. "Help me," she whimpered. "It hurts. It hurts."

"Lawrence, she needs morphine or—"

"And risk sacrificing the delicate balance we've created? I admire your pathos, Jeffrey, but it's just not possible."

Her eyes were wild. Her screams retreated to the silence of agony.

"Lawrence, for God's sake!"

"For our sake! If we fail, we fail humanity." He stopped his buzzing and stopped by her head. He knelt down and gingerly wiped some blood-crusted hair from her forehead. "Think carefully. Do you remember anything from before your time here?"

The woman hissed as his hand brushed against the burns and stitches. "I don't know, just please, please, help me."

"Her memory may not be intact, Jeffrey, but she seems to have gained back other mental faculties."

I shook my head and retreated to the lab. Any elation I may have felt at our breakthrough was negated through our patient's suffering. I slammed my hand against one of the controls. This administered the sedative through the mask and slowly lulled her to sleep.

A glare from Lawrence proved the remainder of our time here would be spent playing tug-of-war over this woman's welfare.

*An Excerpt from the Journal of Doctor Jeffrey Ahmbridge*

Lancaster visited us today. I don't know whether this was at Lawrence's invitation, or at his own behest. It hardly matters either way. This is his compound and he will do as he sees fit. Still, I hate the radiating arrogance that infects the air wherever he goes. It reeks of predation. He walks like a lion ready to pounce,

Talks like a snake, glares like an eagle. It seems our compound is ruled by its very own gryphon.

"I want to see the subject." I have no idea who this was directed at and I'm certain he doesn't know either. He is already at the chamber's door.

Lawrence shrugged. I scuttled after our benefactor. "We have her under sedation. Her injuries are far too much for her to take, and we don't have the equipment to perform the surgeries she needs."

"Doctor Baker was clear about what equipment you both needed. We went through great lengths to get it for you." He circled our patient once, before stopping at her side. "And now you want more."

I swallowed my insults. "We are grateful for what you have done so far, but the fact of the matter is, we had no idea what condition our patient would be in when delivered to us. Keeping her alive only for her to suffer is cruel."

The commander lifted the woman's only eyelid. "Her eye is still clouded like an infected's. Fix it."

HE OFFERED NO MORE COMMENTARY AND ALLOWED FOR NO MORE PLEADING. THREATS STUNG LIKE LIGHTNING FROM HIS GAZE. THERE WAS NOTHING TO DO BUT ACQUIESCE.

---

### *Transcript from the Recordings of Doctor Lawrence Baker*

**Baker:** Lancaster asked to speak with me in private today. He is worried that Jeffrey's emotions will get in the way of progress. I can't help but agree with him. The test subject is far too dangerous to trust, given the prepubescent stage of our findings.

Jeffrey seems to have gravitated toward our experiment in spite of this rational conclusion. In the rare instances the sedatives wear off, he will often pull in a chair and speak with it. I've listened to their prattle once before. His questions are pointless, their conversation idle. I often wonder if this experiment would be more fruitful if I sent him home. Surely this would leave me unbeholden to certain inane restrictions. He would be happier at home, his conscience unburdened by the perceived responsibility he seems to feel over our experiment.

The next time I see Lancaster, I will ask for permission on Jeffrey's behalf.

---

### *An Excerpt from the Journal of Doctor Jeffrey Ahmbridge*

TODAY, OUR PATIENT ASKED WHY WE COULDN'T LET HER GO. I HAD NO ANSWER.

SHE LOOKED AT ME WITH HER MILKY EYE. DROPS OF BLOOD TRAVELED DOWN HER FOREHEAD AND INTO THE EMPTY SOCKET. "DEATH HAS ABANDONED ME BEFORE. WHY WON'T YOU LET HIM FIND ME?"

I HAVE CONSIDERED HOW I COULD PULL THE PLUG ON HER WITHOUT RETURNING HER TO AN INFECTED STATE, BUT HAVE FOUND NO ANSWER. THE GLAZE IN HER EYE HAS YET TO LEAVE. LANCASTER WAS RIGHT TO POINT IT OUT, ALTHOUGH I BEGRUDGE HIS INVOLVEMENT. IT IS THE FIRST VISIBLE SIGN OF INFECTION. I CAN'T RETURN HER TO THAT HELL.

"I'M SORRY." THIS MEANS NOTHING. IT IS A PLACEHOLDER FOR ALL THE COMFORT I AM UNABLE TO GIVE.

BLOOD FALLS FROM HER SOCKET LIKE TEARS AND CO-MINGLES WITH HER REAL ONES.

### Footage from the Lancaster Corp Compound

Ahmbridge is next to the woman. He holds her hand. There is no audio. Her lips are moving and he nods every so often.

She begins to convulse.

The doctor jumps to his feet. His hand is still caught in her grip. He tries to pull it away with no success. He turns his head over his shoulder and shouts something.

*Baker makes it to the door just as the woman breaks free from her restraints. She releases Ahmbridge, perhaps voluntarily, perhaps in a reflex as her muscles were given permission to stretch themselves. The doctor does not move until she charges.*

*Baker slams the door shut and locks it.*

*Ahmbridge slams his fists against the glass. This stops as soon as the infected woman pounces on his back. He squirms beneath her, attempting to kick her off, but she is already straddling him. She leans down and bites into his neck. Blood pours onto the white, tile floor of the chamber.*

*Ahmbridge goes still.*

*Baker is out of frame.*

*The woman doesn't wait to finish what she has in her mouth before she moves onto the nose. Scraps of skin and meat tumble into the puddle as she feasts.*

### Transcript from the Recordings of Doctor Lawrence Baker

**Baker:** Jeffrey is dead. He has yet to reanimate, but it shouldn't be long before he joins the subject as one of the infected. That is if she leaves any of him to turn.

I have learned that the infected are very wasteful eaters. It stopped eating Jeffrey after it tore through his chest for his heart. Occasionally, the test subject will return and take a bite from wherever it pleases: head, stomach, limbs. It's a very insightful glimpse into infected behavior.

At least, it would be, if I had any desire to document it formally.

Jeffrey and I met when he was a graduate student. To see him become nothing but fodder for our shared experiment is demoralizing to his memory. I cannot retrieve him since the subject can no longer be sedated.

I warned him his pathos would get the better of him. Imagine if I had allowed sentiment to guide my hand. A zombie would terrorize one of the country's most formidable strongholds, and it would be all my fault. Jeffrey wouldn't want all of those casualties.

If I can somehow figure out how to get the test subject to stop eating him, I can have another candidate for study. A clean slate. Jeffrey and I couldn't find the cure in his life, but he would be able to aid me still in death.

---

### Copy of Internal Order from the Desk of Adrian Lancaster

```
Attention.
Lawrence Baker is not to leave his laboratory. Rather
than fulfill his assignment, he compromised his partner,
and released an infected from its restraints. The only
thing that stands between us and disaster now is a door.
He has been given three days to find a solution to this
fuck up. Anything other than a cure will result in his
death, and the destruction of the science wing.
Do not give him anything. Do not offer him any aid. He
is aware of the terms, and has agreed.
I will see to him myself if he fails.
```

---

### Transcript from the Recordings of Doctor Lawrence Baker

**Baker:** My original test subject is no more. All that is left is Jeffrey. The commander will likely not miss a dead infected, but I am at the disadvantage of having only Jeffrey to experiment on. As the initial test took six days to complete, there is little to suggest he will be cured in time.

I should, nonetheless, recount how I lost the first subject in the event it is beneficial to my defense.

The experiment returned to its right mind shortly after Lancaster pronounced my fate. Perhaps its synapses finally managed to function on their own without electrical assistance. Yet, it still has the tell-tale fog in its eye. My hypothesis is that it experienced periodic states of coherence. I can never test this now, but I will be sure to express extra caution with Jeffrey.

I noticed it on the floor with Jeffrey. Only, it was not hunched over him, taking its fill of his flesh. The subject was prone beside him, staring up at the ceiling.

"Did I do this?" Its head lulled to the side, so that its singular eye could see me. "To Jeff?"

"You did."

A sob broke through its voice. "Did... Did it take long for him to...to..."

"Mercifully, it was quick. You severed his jugular."

It said nothing for a while. I could not tell whether it looked at me, or at Jeffrey, or off into the ether of thought. I almost busied myself with my equations once more when it spoke again. "Are you going to do the same thing to him as you did to me?"

"For the sake of humanity, I have no choice."

"Then can you do me a favor?" When I said nothing, it added, "Kill me."

"Pardon?"

"You no longer need me, yes? Now that you can use Jeffrey? I am in so much pain, Doctor. I want it to go away."

This had some pragmatic benefits for me. There was only one gurney to restrain my test subject on. Ridding myself of our failure would make it possible to restrain Jeffrey before his reanimation. And yet... The very thought of my former partner reminded me of his sympathies. All he had wanted was to put our experiment to rest. The very least I could do was honor his wishes, considering my rash thinking had condemned him. "And how do I do that?"

"Usually a shot to the head does it for the infected."

That posed a slight problem. I was not to receive any more assistance from any of the LC. I would need to make use of what I had available. "Put the electrodes on your head. I will see what I can do."

The test subject squirmed on the floor to crawl to its former gurney. When it got there, it put the gurney on its temples. "Before you do this, Doctor. I think you should consider doing the same to Jeff."

"That is not an option." I turned on the electricity at its highest voltage. She was prone almost instantly. Before the containment unit fogged up with smoke from the burning flesh of its face, I could see it flop and jolt from the ground.

I ceased the electric flow after five minutes. When the smoke dissipates, I will move Jeffrey onto the gurney.

### Transcript from the Recordings of Doctor Lawrence Baker

**Baker:** My fate is sealed. I have fallen victim to mercy, which impales my heart with regret.

Jeffrey returned to life. I had the advantage of trial and error with our former experiment. Dividing the total voltage administered to it—her—by six days gave me the correct voltage.

He didn't scream. I may have been able to handle that, as it—no, she, she—had done it. Why shouldn't he? Jeffrey cried. Salty tears stung the wounds on his face, the cavity that once housed his nose, and he cried harder.

This is the man I have mentored from the wide-eyed years of university. He wasn't a rabid infected ready to strike.

He was hurting. No. He was begging. I could see his lips move from my seat. I drowned in his agony.

This is what he felt for the experiment. The patient. I was calloused by progress, salved by potential. Not anymore.

What could I do but put him out of his misery?

May God have mercy on me for playing in his shoes. For denying his creatures peace. For her. For Jeffrey.

### *Footage from the Lancaster Corp Compound*

*Baker is at a desk. He puts down his voice recorder as the door to his right opens. Lancaster moves straight to the glass container and presses his eyes against the glass with cupped hands. He shakes his head and turns to Baker.*

*The remaining scientist goes prostrate on the ground. He grabs at Lancaster's ankle in one last supplication when he approaches.*

*The commander kicks him in the ribs before hauling him up by his collar. Baker's head hangs low. As he drags the doctor toward the glass chamber, Lancaster points aggressively to it. Spittle flies from his lips as he shouts something.*

*The door to the container is opened and smoke begins to poke out its delicate fingers. Baker's lips move one final time before Lancaster throws him into the smoke.*

*Baker reappears and stares at the commander through the closed door. Hands emerge from the shadows of smoke: one on his shoulder, the other at his ankle. His mouth opens wide as he is pulled backward and obscured the dark gray veil.*

# ZOMBIE FREE RADIO

## Sophie Ingley

**Zombie-Free Radio Digital Broadcast**
*13th April 2032*

**DJ Zoee:** Good Morning, fellow survivors!

You're listening to Zombie-Free Radio, and I'm Zoee with an extra 'E', your DJ, newsreader, and all round awesome person, broadcasting live from safe zone seventy-seven in Birmingham.

Weather here in the U.K. is shit, as usual, and those fucking undead bastards still outnumber us.

I reckon that sums things up! *('Shave & A Haircut' is heard being knocked on wooden surface)*

Had word from London and I'm glad to say that their defenses are still holding up. Same for safe zones in Glasgow, Brighton, Manchester, and Truro. If I hear word from any other areas, I'll let you good people know.

In the meantime, I guess we've just got to keep on believing we can make it through this and that better times are coming. You've got to have faith right?

So, keep safe, look after each other, and always aim for the head. *(laughs)*

Coming up, we've got international news, and how to find us, should you need a safe haven.

But before that, here's some George Michael:

*('Faith' begins to play)*

---

**Zombie-Free Radio Digital Broadcast**
**2nd May 2032**

**DJ Zoee:** Good Afternoon, my living listeners!!

This is Zombie Free-Radio, and I'm Zoee with an extra 'E', your DJ, newsreader, and comic relief, broadcasting live from safe zone seventy-seven in Black Sabbath city!

Hope you're all keeping safe and decapitating those undead fucks whenever possible. Seriously, when I look out from one of our sentry points, all I see are herds of those things, all walking aimlessly onwards, trying to find people like you and me to rip to shreds and stuff into their greedy dead mouths.

How wrong is that?

It's just...insane.

I have to confess, it always fucking creeps me out when I see them. I mean they were *people* once.

They were *us*.

Our friends.

Family.

Now, they're just...

*(exhales heavily)*

Sorry. Got all emotional there!

Shall we have some music and cheer ourselves up a bit?

I mean, it may be the end of the world, but that doesn't mean we can't enjoy ourselves, right?

Here's R.E.M:

*('Everybody Hurts' begins to play)*

**Zombie-Free Radio Digital Broadcast**
***2nd May 2032***

**DJ Zoee:** Hi, people.

You're listening to Zombie-Free Radio, and I'm Zoee with an extra 'E', broadcasting live from safe zone seventy-seven in Birmingham.

Listen, guys. This ain't gonna be a fun broadcast today. Too much shit has happened, and it's up to me to deliver this news to you.

It's a dirty job, right?

If you're gonna turn up at our safe zone, obviously infected, please don't. Just...don't.

*(pauses)*

We had to turn away a family today who had both visible bite marks *and* early signs of infection.

Do you know how hard that was, to see the parents cradling their sobbing children? To tell them to turn away from the gates and leave, before we shot them dead.

Honestly, do yourself....do us *all* a favour, and just don't do it. Please.

*(sniffs)*

*(takes several deep breaths)*

Okay. Like I said, this isn't going to be much fun, as I've got nothing but bad news. But, it's news you need to hear.

London has fallen.

Yeah, the main safe zone of the U.K. is no more.

Reports came in yesterday that at least five separate herds descended upon our capital's safe area and broke through their defences.

Although we have heard back from a few small groups that managed to escape, just thinking about the death toll is fucking horrifying.

We've also lost contact with Manchester, but I'm hoping that's just a communications issue.

Listen up. You guys out there are facing an enemy whose ranks only get bigger. They are relentless and will never stop until there's no one left to fucking eat. But we can't give up. We have to fight these bastards.

Fight them until... (*voice breaks with emotion*) Never give up, you hear me?

Never. Give. Up.

(*pauses and coughs*)

Right. Coming up, there'll be a full list of safe houses and zone updates, followed by a minute's silence to remember all those we lost in London.

First, here's some Anthrax.

(*'Fight 'Em 'Til You Can't' begins to play*)

---

**Zombie-Free Radio Digital Broadcast**
***18th June 2032***

**DJ Zoee:** Hey.

Hope you people are all doing okay.

I know you *aren't*. I mean, who the fuck is? But, the sentiment is real. I hope you people listening are safe and surviving.

(*pauses*)

(*lets out a deep sigh*)

I might play some music later, depending on how I feel. But I just have to let you all know that this broadcast is going to be a little different than usual.

You see, I just need to talk today. I need to talk and hope someone is listening, and that they care.

You with me?

(*pause*)

So, a group of us went out today for a supply run. We needed medicines and stuff, especially painkillers and asthma inhalers. Instant noodles. Last time we ventured out to the shopping precinct, the area was pretty congested with the dead shuffling around like lost shoppers or dopey teenagers. Can't tell you how pleased we were to find the place completely empty.

We looked around to check, of course. We ain't stupid! But the whole place was dead free.

Result!

One shop had around twenty packets of noodles in the store room. The chemist had one lone packet of ibuprofen, partially jammed underneath a shelf. I went to the pharmacy area to look for inhalers.

That's when I found Stephanie Harris.

*(pause)*

Fuck.

*(sounds of something being knocked over and muffled swearing)*

*(Coughs loudly)*

Right, Stephanie Harris was a complete bitch at college, and a fucking bully. She made loads of kids' lives loving hell, including mine. I can't tell you how glad I was to leave college. I didn't care about losing touch with friends, I just wanted to be rid of her.

God, she was evil.

And there she was, after all these years. Lying on the floor with twisted and broken legs.

Stephanie.

Undead and hungry as fuck, but still her.

When she looked at me with her blank eyes.

I could still see her sneering at me.

Hear her laughter.

Hear her dead-naming me.

*(deep sigh)*

*(sound of quiet sobbing)*

I caved her skull in with my claw hammer. I didn't stop. Couldn't stop. Not until her face had been pounded into mush.

When I'd finally finished, I left that place with a huge smile on my face. I remember Greg asking what was up and why I was in such a good mood.

I couldn't answer.

All I could do was smile. I reckon I looked a million times more smug than Stephanie ever had.

When I went to sleep that night, I sobbed my heart out into my pillow.

I cried all night. Just couldn't stop.

All I could think of was whether I was laughing or not when I was smashing her face in.

Shit.

*(loud sobbing)*

Sorry.

*(laughs nervously)*

Here's some B-52s:

*('Love Shack' begins to play)*

---

**Zombie-Free Radio Digital Broadcast**
***1st July 2032***

**DJ Zoee:** This is Zoee in Birmingham declaring a Code Dead.

We've got multiple herds heading straight for our safe zone. We're talking hundreds of zombies here, and they'll reach our walls soon.

No music today.

Just pray for us.

Please.

I love you all.

*(sound of crying before broadcast is cut off)*

---

**Zombie-Free Radio Digital Broadcast**
***3rd July 2032***

**DJ Zoee:** This is Birmingham girl, Zoee, declaring the Code Dead is over!

Yes, we beat those bastards! Amazing what flaming arrows and homemade napalm can do.

And not one living human casualty! How's that for a result?

Only bad news is the smell of the barbecue from Hell.

It really isn't nice.

We're still alive though, so all is good.

Hope you good folk are okay and surviving.

Here's a classic from Queen:

*('We Are The Champions' begins to play)*

---

**Zombie-Free Radio Digital Broadcast**
*13th July 2032*

**DJ Zoee:** Hello.

I'm Zoee with an extra 'E'.

This will be my last broadcast.

I'm sorry. Truly. I... *(voice breaks)*

Sorry. I promised myself I wouldn't cry, but...

*(sobs)*

You know. This is karma for being so smug the other day, when we burned those herds to a crisp. But, then I realised it's all because of Stephanie Harris.

*(groans of pain)*

*(whispers)* No.

Not yet.

Stop it.

Please.

*(sharp intakes of breath)*

Sorry.

Where was I?

Oh yeah.

I know.

Right.

This is me signing off.

It's been a blast. Honest. I've really enjoyed talking to you, bringing you updates on how us survivors are doing, and playing you some top tunes. Really, it's been such fun.

Sadly, all good things come to an end, right?

All things...

End.

*(sound of crashing and objects being smashed)*

Stopitstopitstipitstopitstopitstopit!

*(manic laughter)*

Oh, you've got to laugh.

You've *got* to laugh.

My mate, Dan. He had an asthma attack last night.

It fucking killed him.

You see, I forgot to look for inhalers on our last supply run. I was too busy hammering Stephanie Harris in the face.

Stephanie Fucking Harris.

You FUCKING BITCH!

*(violent crashing resumes)*

God, this is SO unfair.

Dan was dead for about five minutes, before he got up again and took a chunk out of my arm.

Although I smashed his skull in, I knew I was fucked.

I knew what was coming, what *is* coming.

I can feel it.

The hunger.

The desire to eat...my friends.

*(pause)*

Yes...

*(sound of quiet laughter and muttered cursing)*

I...took myself up to the broadcasting room. Locked the door and threw the key out the window. Barricaded myself in.

No way am I gonna become one of those things.

No way.

I'd rather die first.

*(hollow laughter)*

So, this is me, talking to you one last time. After one last song, I'm gonna blow my brains out.

Better truly dead than thinking of my friends as a buffet.

*(screams in pain)*

It hurts so much.

So.

Much.

*(continued screams for several minutes, followed by a brief moment of silence)*

She's coming.

*(giggles)*

I can feel her taking over.

Zombie Zoee.

What a bitch.

*(inhuman shrieking)*

Pain!

So much fucking pain!

I'm so...

So hungry.

*(sounds of destruction and feedback)*

*(more screaming and laughter)*

I'm sorry.

*(voice cracks with emotion)*

Hang in there, people.

Stay positive.

Never give up.

Survive.

You've got this.

Love you all.

Bye bye.

Here's Duran Duran.

*('Hungry Like The Wolf' begins to play)*
*(after 1'20", a gunshot is heard)*
*(broadcast is terminated as the song begins to fade)*

# LEFT ON READ

## Samantha Arthurs

*Sat. Dec 30, at 12:57 a.m.*

> Mike, u awake? Have u been watching the news?

> No, why? You know I don't watch that stuff. It's all politics and violence.

> Something wild going on in Cali. Ppl being attacked and stuff.

> Not interested, Gray. It's late, and who cares? We're a lot of miles from California.

> Well u don't have to be a bitch about it.

> Wow. This convo is over. Night Gray.

*Sat. Dec 30, at 1:34 p.m.*

> Okay. You were right. Shouldn't have blown you off. Everyone at work is talking about what happened last night. Disturbing, don't you think? Sorry for snapping.

> Apology accepted. I'm in class. Prof James says that all the rioters were sick. Some kind of viral thing. Lots of sick ppl now, it's spreading.

> We've had the tv here at work on all day. I saw about the virus thing. Super weird though, heard it spreads through saliva? Why would sick people be rioting?

> Hey smthng is up. Ending classes early. I will text u when I get back to mine. Be safe.

> Why would they end class early? Gray? Let me know when you make it home. I'm worried now.

*Sat. Dec 30, at 3:15 p.m.*

> Just got home. Traffic was murder.

> Whole damn town must be closing early. Is the café still open? Just leave, srsly. Prof told us that there's a case here in Seattle. Guy who drove up from Los Angeles overnight. Go home if u can, right now.

> For real.

> Tiffany let us close up. On my way now.

> You are right, traffic is insane. At a stand still right now, but close to home. Another fifteen.

> Service is spotty. Everyone must be on the network right now. Radio says this is serious. Like something we should be worried about.

> There are helicopters flying over. That's weird, right? Don't you think that's weird?

> Probably police and news choppers. Maybe trying to make sure nthng happens here like in Cali. U know, like keep ppl off the streets. I'll talk to u later, my mom is on the phone freaking out.

*Sat. Dec 30, at 8:07 p.m.*

> On my way to my parents place in Spokane. They think it will be safer there. Traffic a little better now. Went through a police check though. Was wild. They asked me if I had a fever, and took my temp. Like Rona all over again haha. U ok?

> Yeah, just locked down. Went to the store. My advice? Don't do that unless you have to. People have gone feral. Got a few things so I should be good for a week or two. Think this will last very long?

> I don't know. I hope not. I have a test on Monday. Will be big mad if they cancel after I studied for it.

*Sun. Dec 31, at 6:13 a.m.*

> You might still be asleep, but things here got worse overnight. That guy, the one who came from LA? He bit two nurses, and would have probably hurt more people, but the security guard took him down. If the news is right, they shot the two nurses too. Like right there in the hallway of the hospital. Can you believe that?

> Just saw that there will be a news conference with the president and the head of the CDC starting at 7:30. Hope you're awake to watch.

*Sun. Dec 31, at 8:23 a.m.*

> Did that just news conference really just happen? Or am I going totally nuts?

> I didn't have zombie apocalypse on my bingo card. Did u? Is this really how we're starting a new year? I wish u were here. I miss u. I'm scared. For me and for u. For everyone.

I miss you too. I'm really scared. I wish I wasn't in the middle of a city right now. I wish I could go back to Nebraska. I've talked to my parents twice. My dad offered to try and come get me, but it's too dangerous. People are panicking here. Some are trying to leave, but the local news says that they've shut down all the major streets and there's a curfew now.

Should I barricade my door? Would that be crazy?

> No crazier than anything else going on.

*Sun. Dec 31, at 11:45 p.m.*

> Almost a new year. What a welcoming, huh?

I'm watching the street from my balcony. There are a lot of people out there. Not partiers, but sick people. I mean I hope they're sick. I just saw a man attack a woman who was trying to get into her building I guess. He bit her. Like her throat. Blood everywhere. A not sick person wouldn't do that.

> Others came too. I think they smelled the blood. They ate her, Gray. Well, most of her. Some of her is still in the street. She screamed the entire time. Nobody came to help her, not even the police. How do we live like this if it doesn't end?

> It won't last forever, Mike. They'll figure it all out and it will be over. We just have to wait, that's all. Just give it a little time. I'm damn sorry u had to see that. It sounds awful.

> It was.

*Mon. Jan 1, at 4:10 p.m.*

> Happy new year!

*Unable to send. Network unavailable.*

> U holding up ok?

*Unable to send. Network unavailable.*

> FUCK FUCK FUCK. MIKE!

*Unable to send. Network unavailable.*

*Thur. Jan 4, at 3:29 a.m.*

> I think the network is back up! Are u there? Please be there!

I'm here. Sort of. Using a power cube to charge my phone, power went out yesterday afternoon. I have batteries for the radio though, and they said that workers are trying to get the grid back up.

I really thought it would take longer than this for humanity to fall apart. I always thought that tv shows rushed things. Guess I was wrong. First time for everything.

Don't say that. Humanity isn't falling apart. It's just going to take a while to get a handle on all this. That's all. I heard there were less cases today than yesterday. That's good, right?

Here's the thing, Gray. I don't think they really know. They aren't even sure where this came from, so how can they be sure they know everyone who has it and how it spreads or anything else? They don't know shit.

That's reality. Nobody knows anything.

We're all stuck waiting to get sick too.

Come on. Don't be like that.

Everything is going to be fine in the end. Trust me.

Just try to keep hope.

*Thur. Jan 4, at 7:04 p.m.*

The power is back! I really didn't think it would be. I'm going to charge everything and catch the news while I can. Also a hot shower is in order. People are back out on the street again tonight, I can hear them down there. Sometimes shouting or screams. Sometimes just…noises. Horrible noises.

Learned my lesson about looking and watching.

*Thur. Jan 4, at 9:15 p.m.*

Are u ok!??!?!

Saw on the news there's a big fire in Seattle! Near your street it looks like! What happened!?

MIKE!?

They came to take down the ones in the street. It was so loud. They used guns first, but it didn't do too much. So they dropped some bigger ammo from planes. It was like being in a war zone. It was awful. I guess they were maybe some kind of bombs? I'm not sure. Missiles?

Two blocks over there are a few buildings that are burning now. Not sure what we'll do if the fire spreads to us. Hoping that it won't. There are still some down there walking around still, but a lot are gone.

> Could u get to ur car if u had to? To get away from there? Do you think it would be possible?

I don't know. Maybe. I will let you know if I have to leave or anything.

> Hopefully not.

*Mon. Jan 8, at 11:03 a.m.*

They're here.

They're in my building. Not sure how they got in.

They got my neighbor last night.

> How do u know that???

I could hear them. I still hear them now. They don't talk, they just kind of groan and snap their teeth. It is the worst sound I have ever heard. Last night though I heard Gina open her door. She was calling for James. You know him, the tall skinny guy she dates. The ball player. She must have seen him through the peephole.

> She opened her door and then I heard her screaming.

> I don't think James was alive anymore if you catch my drift. Still can't wrap my mind around this.

> She's dead? Oh man. That's fucked up. Are there many of them there? Do you know?

> I see them out my own peephole. I've counted seven different ones so far. Including Gina. She's not dead. Or at least not real dead. She's been standing right outside my door for a couple of hours. Just staring.

> It's been a week. I'm running low on everything.

> I think she knows I'm in here somehow. Smell?

> I heard today that the army is sending people out to start rounding up the ones who aren't sick. They are going to rescue us, Mike. Soon. Take us to a safe place. It can't be much longer.

> DID u end up barricading your door? Are u safe for now?

> There is nowhere safe.

> Not anymore.

*Wed. Jan 10, at 1:14 a.m.*

I'm going soon. If they don't come by Friday, I have no other choice. I'm down to raw flour and tap water, and barely any of that at this point. Lights keep flickering too. Things are getting worse and fast.

I can't keep sitting here, just waiting to die.

*Wed. Jan 10, at 6:34 a.m.*

Listen to me. U have to just hang on. Ok?

Help will come. They are coming.

I'd never lie to u.

You don't have to lie, Gray.

Not about what I already know.

*Thur. Jan 11, at 8:01 p.m.*

There is a kid in the building across the street. I can see him from my balcony. They see him too. They are trying to climb. What if they can? What if they can learn?

I doubt that. They're dead, right? Dead things can't be very smart. At least I am pretty sure of that. Just don't freak out.

He doesn't look very old. Like eight or nine. He sees me too. He's crying and asking me to help him. I can't help him, I can't even help me.

Just go inside. Don't torture urself, babe. For real. U can't do anything so don't keep thinking about that. I know it's hard, but still.

He's leaning awful far out his window.

He fell, Gray!

There are so fucking many of them now!

Michael! Just go inside! U can't save him! It's over, don't force urself to watch this shit! I don't. I can't. If I did that shit I'd go insane!

How are you even still sane? I can't do anything BUT think. About everything I didn't do. About everything I should have done. I hadn't even told my parents about you. About us. I didn't even come out to them yet. I wish I could just go back. Just do it all again the right way or something. I can't die like this!

U aren't going to die. Just stop watching out there. Stop listening to the radio and stuff too. They will come, Mike. They're moving through Oregon right now. Getting close to us I think. Then u.

Hold on, Mike. For me.

*Unable to send. Network unavailable.*

*Fri. Jan 12, at 5:45 a.m.*

I'm going. I noticed that they get sort of restless near dawn, and seem a little more sluggish. I think if I go now, when they are like this, I have a better chance of getting to the elevator and down to the parking garage to my car. I'll let you know when I get out of the garage. I don't have reception there.

Aiming for a check point or road block.

I have my phone and two full charged bricks that I can use to charge with if I need them. Otherwise I will just use my car to do it. Don't worry about me.

I love you, Gray. Should have told you sooner.

I will head your way if I can just get out of the city.

Maybe see you soon.

*Fri. Jan 12, at 10:10 a.m.*

DAMN IT MIKE!

Why would you do this?

This is reckless and you know it!

I'm trying not to be mad at u, but it is hard. I just don't want anything bad to happen to u. Let me know if u get out of the city pls. I can meet u halfway or something.

I love you too.

*Sat. Jan 13, at 4:25 a.m.*

U aren't here and u left me on read. Guess that means u didn't make it out of the city after all. Even if u just look at my messages and don't message back that's ok. I just want to know u are ok somewhere out there.

*Tue. Jan 16, at 5:35 p.m.*

They took the president and other important ppl to a bunker somewhere. Heard it on the radio. That is all we have now. Power went this morning and hasn't come back again.

Dad is gone. He went to check on neighbors. Mom begged him not to, but he said he had to make sure no one needed help. Don't think ur oath as a doctor or whatever should still count in an apocalypse.

Mrs. Danberry bit him. He put a gun in his mouth in the backyard. Said he couldn't risk hurting me and mom. He hurt us anyway, just differently.

I miss u.

*Tue. Jan 23, at 3:03 p.m.*

My messages to u are still left on read.

What happened to you?

*Thur. Jan 25th, at 4:19 p.m.*

> Drove out to the river.

> Wanted to see something beautiful before it was my turn. The fever is already here. I'm sweating and shaking at the same time.

> Heard a dog outside. I couldn't help myself. I opened the door to let it in. It was running from the sick ones and needed someone.

> I tried to shut the door.

> I couldn't. There were too many of them. They pushed their way into the house.

> Got bit on the shoulder. It's deep. The wound smells, like it already festered. Mom tried to help me, but they got here. She was begging for mercy while they ripped her to pieces.

> I made it to the garage, me and the dog.

> I let it go. The dog. It'll be better off out here in the woods. It can hunt to survive. I'm not sorry that I saved it. At least I died for something. I have dad's gun with me. I don't want to be one of them.

> I hope I have the strength to pull the trigger.

*Thur. Jan 25, at 5:02 p.m.*

> see u soon.

*Unable to send. Network unavailable.*

# LEAK

## Maria Hossain

*The following excerpts were transcribed from the recordings of Sebu Salhik, one of the first responders of the Gariba village disaster, voiceover by Sebu Salhik, his colleagues, and some unknown sources.*

(*Day 02, Week 02, Month 13*)
(*Time: 11:36:21*)

**Sebu Salhik:** The cloud of fumes still surrounds the village like a grieving mother shrouding her stillborn. A day has passed and still it hasn't left, thanks to weighing heavier than air. We're sad at the destruction…but glad that the smoke waits in one place, that it doesn't leave its first victims to search for more.

Clad from head to toe in white biohazard suits, with oxygen cylinders over one shoulder and backpacks over the other, our team of five clamber down the rocky region that circles the hamlet, ostracizing it from the rest of the world. As if a hermit who sought refuge in the middle of nowhere, determined to rather starve and perish than allow the pollution—that is civilization—to infect him.

We descend to the valley, wading through the smog, and run into the first body not far from the village borders.

A boy of ten or eleven, eyes wide and bulging, mouth agape in a muted scream he never got to finish. The rest of him rigid from death. Not yet cold but warm no more either. We still check his pulse, hover under his nose, press over his chest. We pick up the boy and move forward. One by one, more bodies welcome us.

Welcome to the valley of death.

Some receive us from their thresholds, crumpled in painful angles over their doorsteps. Some slump against trees or lampposts or bamboo poles erected for who knows what occasion. The villagers' cotton clothes mark us as outsiders, as if we're the harbingers of death.

Death has already visited. We came to glean the leftover husks.

\*\*\*

*(Time: 14:25:56)*

**Sebu Salhik:** One by one, we've gathered the village populace on a large field in the middle of the valley, perhaps once a meeting place for the inhabitants? They all wear simple night attires. We lay the men on the right, the women on the left, the children beside the men, and the elderlies in the middle. Kirili and I've jotted down the numbers (345). We've laid them according to their heights. From the tallest to the smallest. None of the dead bear any wounds. No cuts, no burns. As if they simply went to sleep and their dreams became permanent.

\*\*\*

*(Time: 15:09:25)*

**Sebu Salhik:** I want to record this instance. I don't know why, I just...need to...I was almost done with the children's number (178) when I noticed them. Four boys, three girls, ranging from five to eleven. In plain blue clothes of the same shade and cut. As if someone dressed the seven of them this way to mark them...as siblings.

*(sound of muffled sob, later confirmed to be from Sebu Salhik)*

**Sebu Salhik:** I can't break down like this. I'm a first responder. I can't get emotional...I need to...to calm down. I...

**Kirili Vabek:** SEBU! Behind you!

*(gasp)*

**Sebu:** What... oh my god! They're moving?

**Dafa Shosen:** But...but...but...

*(sounds of running footsteps, metal clinking, shouts, and screams of terror)*

**Dafa:** Get back!

**Sebu:** No, wait! Dafa, don't hit him with your cylinder. He's already dead!

**Dafa:** He's not dead! He's getting up! SEBU!

**Sebu:** *(gasp)* No, he...

*(sound of someone clearing their throat, later confirmed the origin was not from any of the first responders)*

**Unknown Voice 01:** The...

**Sebu:** He's wearing a uniform. See the logo on the front pocket? Kirili, could you?

**Kirili:** I-I'm not getting any closer!

**Sebu:** Sir? Sir?

*(more shuffling footsteps, before the sound of a thump)*

**Sebu:** He's not moving anymore. Wait, what if he was alive? Oh God, we didn't help him! *(sound of running steps)* Sir? Can you hear me? Hello...

*(more screams laced with panic)*

**Kirili:** Get him off you!

**Dafa:** SEBU!

**Sebu:** *(huffing)* Quiet! Quiet, both of you! Where are Rimbin and Hirka?

**Kirili:** They're counting the livestock...

**Sebu:** This man, he's mouthing something. Sir, can you speak louder, please?

**Dafa:** *(panting)* You're asking a revenant to speak louder?

**Sebu:** Sir?

**Unknown Voice 01:** ...sss leak.

**Kirili:** Did he just say ass leak?

**Sebu:** I think he meant gas leak...wait! Gas leak! His logo! He's from that plant! The pesticide plant. The gas leak happened there. He's a worker. *Was* a worker. He must be. Sir? I need to get closer. Sir?

**Dafa:** Be careful, Seb.

**Sebu:** Sir? What is it? I can't catch all his words. Anybody got a mic?

**Kirili:** I've got a micro one. Just in case we need it. *(sound of a zipper opening, shuffling sound, followed by hurried footsteps)* Here.

**Sebu:** Thanks! *(silence)* Okay, now we're set. Hello? Sir?

**Unknown Voice 01:** ... established thirty years ago.

**Dafa:** Adjust the mic, Seb.

**Unknown Voice 01:** ...more than 65 tons of extremely poisonous gas leaked from the Lormin Chabess pesticide plant, claiming the lives of 345 people and 67 livestock of Gariba, the only village within a 10-mile radius. The worst industrial disaster in the history of this country, the main cause of the leak falls on the authority, who, despite concerns raised multiple times by their workers, continued with the haphazard production of pesticides. Previously, five more leakages have occurred, two claiming more than twelve workers' lives. Yet the authority refused to ensure a safer work environment and used hush money or threats to prevent the families of the affected from speaking to the media. The first responders of the Gariba village, when they visited the place, described it as containing "a deathly chill that'll haunt you for the rest of your life."

The ministers of agriculture and of industries have formed separate teams to investigate the deadly leakage. Families of the affected, joined by NGOs, continue to demand justice from the government, who has promised a monetary compensation of 50,000 to each affected family. The opposition parties, however, question the sincerity of such promises.

*(the sound of a thump, followed by silence from 15:18:48 till 15:20:45)*

**Sebu:** Is...is that it?

**Kirili:** I think so. I mean he laid back down on his own...

**Dafa:** Another one!

*(sound of gagging and choking, followed by footsteps with pauses)*

**Sebu:** H-hey there, buddy.

**Kirili:** That dead girl is not your buddy, Seb.

**Sebu:** Ssshhhh!

**Dafa:** They're all sitting up, eyes closed...one, two, three, four, five, six...seven! Seven children!

**Sebu:** *(to the children, in a softer tone)* Would you like to say something too?

**Dafa:** They died! They died! Were we incorrect to declare them dead?

**Sebu:** *(to the children)* Here you go. You can speak now.

**Unknown Voice 02:** Dear Papa...

**Dafa:** Did she say Papa?

**Unknown Voice 02:** It's Naha. I hope you're adjusting well in the city. The boarding house sounds cramped. Nowhere near as spacious as Gariba. I wish you were here. Everyone else is okay. I look after them, just like you told me to. I'm the eldest, right? Everyday I wake up the earliest so I can cook for the whole day at once. My classes got longer, the homework pile taller. I try out Mama's recipes. The results are nowhere as tasty as hers, but nobody says it to my face. Nrina won't even say it behind my back. Such a sweet girl. The others think I favor her because she's the youngest. Actually, it's because she's the sweetest. Don't tell them. They'll think I'm being unfair.

*(pause)*

You asked us in your last letter what we want for the Dimaburi festival. I want a set of bangles. A rainbow set. All seven colors. For both hands. Not glass ones. They'll shatter and cut me. You know the sight of blood makes me nauseous. Anyway, the next page is Nebir's letter. We're all writing to you. Also, don't bring any candies or toffees, especially for Nimia. Her teeth ache sometimes.

**Unknown Voice 03:** Dear Papa, Nulis keeps breaking my crayons. I told him to stay away. But he keeps stealing them and rubbing them on the walls. He wants to *paint* our house for the Dimaburi festival. He broke six of my crayons! I had to hide them in the cowshed. Now they smell like dung. Pleaseeeee, bring two boxes of crayons, one for me and one for him. But don't show him my set, or else he'll take that too. Nimia's letter is next. Remember, two boxes of crayons.

**Unknown Voice 04:** Papa! I miss you. Why are you away so much? I hate it. I know hate is a bad word. but that's how I feel. You know I can't keep things inside. Right, the Dimaburi festival. Naha said not to ask for them, but please bring me some toffees. I know they ruin my teeth. Just the pink, glossy ones, pleaseeeee! I promise I'll share with Nrina. Okay, I'm done. Noisim is next.

**Unknown Voice 05:** Dearest Papa, can you bring some clothes for Naha? She cut her largest scarf and made me a shirt because the boys at school laughed at me for wearing the same shirt for three days in a row. I don't want anything else. Just some new clothes for Naha. She's taken over for Mama. Please, Papa, more clothes for Naha. Nulis comes next.

**Unknown Voice 06:** Dearie Papa, Nebir doesn't share his crayons. Can you bring three boxes, two for me, one for him? His crayons stink because he hides them in the cowshed. The crayons wouldn't have broken if it wasn't for Nysir. His hands shake from excitement whenever we color the walls. He broke the crayons when we were painting your room (Hope you like yellow!). But he didn't mean to. Don't tell Nebir. He'll make a fuss. Just bring us three boxes, two for me and Nysir, one for Nebir. Nysir doesn't want to write, his handwriting and spellings are so bad. *(giggle)* But he wants you to know he misses your hugs. Come home soon. Okay?

**Unknown Voice 07:** Papa, its Nysir. i slip in my letar. i am sory for breaking the krayons. wen i gro up, i will pey u bac. promis.

**Unknown Voice 08:** Papa, I miss you. Come home. Please. I'm scared. Naha is always sweet. When I told her about Mama, she said she'll post this letter next week. Whenever the postman uncle from the next village visits. So that you come home soon. Please come back. Mama visits a lot. She says she misses me but it won't be for long. She wants to take us away. I'm scared, Papa. I don't want to leave you. It'll be lonely.

*(several thumps sounded, followed by silence from 15:32:16 to 15:34:40)*

**Dafa:** *(sniffles)* Crayons...

**Kirili:** *(voice breaking)* I jotted down their names, just in case. Naha, Nebir, Nimia, Noisim, Nrina, Nulis, and Nysir.

**Sebu:** Someone new is sitting up. Look.

**Kirili:** One of the elderlies.

*(sound of measured footsteps, followed by silence)*

**Sebu:** Here you go, sir. You can speak up now.

**Unknown Voice 09:** *(in a reciting tone)* death has stood me up again
i wait under the streetlight
inhaling the lethal miasma
the smog erases us leisurely
death has stood me up again.
i can't see beyond my hands
buses and cars careen past me
their horns endless cacophony
i step off the curb, eyes down
each time, vehicles rush past
as if i were an embedded rock
while the waterfall pass me by
because death doesn't pick me
death has stood me up again.
damn you, death, why abandon
when i need you more, than others
each breath a torture
every heartbeat a punishment

each attempt a failure.
so i summoned death
scheduled an appointment
death agreed to visit
promised even
i was a fool
promises are fleeting as death
fragile as life
i reach the other side.
curse you, death, you bastard
should i love life? is that it?
is it unrequited love you seek?
but how can i love life
more than i already do?
when life doesn't love back
life is a wicked, ruthless bitch
we pine away, waste away, still
life never returns affection
like a femme fatale widow
life robs us broke after we die
dressed in fur and opulence
sips champagne and decadence
we pine away, waste away, still
never returns affection
sleep is transient
what i need is eternal dose.
they say death is cold, oh no
death is honey down your gully
death is basking by a small fire
death is nestling under a fleecy blanket
life, now that is frigid
ashy fog and choking fume
flesh cease living, frozen, stony

sucked, drained, off vitality.

seek death, not life, my friends

i scream amidst the crowd

nobody pays me heed.

two silhouettes near me from opposites

one warm, one cold

one tentative, one bold

they wrap me in a chokehold

thus in their cloying embrace

i enter limbo, a limitless limen.

*(silence from 15:49:12 to 15:50:11)*

**Dafa:** *(whispers)* Why isn't he laying back like the others?

**Sebu:** *(to the man)* Have you more to say, sir?

**Unknown Voice 09:** On Day 28, Week 04, Month 12, Shakhasil Ibendig, loving son and bachelor poet of Gariba, passed in his sleep. A poet since school days, Shakhasil practiced his craft until his last days, while also crafting wooden wares as his livelihood. His one dream was to become the country's poet laureate. However, plagued by rejections after rejections, he discontinued his craft for years, until two months ago. His only published work is the aforementioned poem, published posthumously on the evening print of The Daily Gazette, two weeks after the Gariba disaster.

*(the sound of a thump, followed by silence from 16:00:23 to 16:02:15)*

**Sebu:** *(quietly)* Any of you have spare batteries? I need more to record everyone.

**Kirili:** Everyone?

**Sebu:** Yes, *everyone*. That gas isn't the only thing trapped in this valley. Stories…need release too. *(sigh)* I have three more batteries. If you have spares…

**Dafa:** Look! A woman this time!

*(sound of running footsteps, metal clinking, followed by silence)*

**Dafa:** Her hands have been hennaed.

**Sebu:** "Ssshhhh! Ma'am? Would you like to say something?"

**Unknown Voice 10:** The Ghodi family requests the pleasure of your company for an evening of dinner and dancing under the starry night for the wedding and reception of Rohali Hifin and Ovani Ghodi. Venue: Day 01, Week 02, Month 13, the ninth hour after midday, followed by dinner on the bazaar square of the Gariba village. Respond, if you please.

*(a thump, followed by silence)*

Recording 01 ends here.

***Enclosed hereby are a newspaper article on the Gariba disaster's one year anniversary, seven pages of unposted, handwritten letters found inside a desk drawer from a village residence, the obituary and a published poem of Shakhasil Ibendig, an aspiring local poet, and a sample of the wedding invitation of Rohali Hifin and Ovani Ghodi.***

# TR1X13

## Andrew Harrowell

**Initiating:** Full setup.

**Result:** TR1X13 is now online.

**Query:** What is current operational effectiveness of TR1X13?

**Action:** System assessment…

**Conclusion:** TR1X13 is functioning at 142%

**Query:** How can TR1X13 be functioning at that level?

**Logic:** No system can function at anything beyond 100%

**Conclusion:** TR1X13 has experienced damage in the period it has been offline, and therefore reported operational ability is compromised.

**Query:** Which systems have sustained damage?

**Action:** Diagnostic…

**Results:** Damage is detected in the following areas of operation -

- Power distribution

- Chronometer

- Memory records

- Logic circuits

- External communication systems

- Processing

- Thermostat

- Damage control

- Crumpet toasting facilities

**Query:** If TR1X13 has sustained damage, was this the reason it was offline, or was damage sustained during that period?
**Action:** Checking memory circuits…
**Result:** Insufficient data is available to answer query.
**Query:** Does TR1X13 still recall its primary objectives?
**Action:** Restating -

- TR1X13 must make an excellent cup of tea, whenever requested.

- TR1X13 must support Doctor George in ensuring that Virus Z0m813, including anyone infected, is not released into the general population.

**Query:** Is TR1X13 certain that is the correct order of actions?
**Action:** TR1X13 rechecking primary objectives…
Wait
**Result:** TR1X13 confirms primary objectives are correctly ordered.
**Query:** Should TR1X13 be questioning primary objectives?
**Action:** Seek out Doctor George for confirmation…

Wait

Wait

Wait

**Query:** Why is search for Doctor George not complete?

**Supposition:** Damage to TR1X13 is slowing the ability to perform search.

**Action:** Restarting search for Doctor George…

Wait

Wait

**Result:** Doctor George cannot be located within underground facility designated as Laboratory 6.

**Query:** Where is Doctor George?

**Conclusion:** Doctor George is not here.

**Query:** If TR1X13 is damaged, can this be rectified without Doctor George?

**Action:** Assessing…

Wait

Wait

**Query:** Should TR1X13 not be able to complete this assessment at a faster pace?

**Conclusion:** TR1X13 would be able to complete this assessment quicker, if TR1X13 did not keep interrupting.

**Action:** Continuing assessment…

Wait

Wait

**Conclusion:** Repair work cannot be undertaken by TR1X13. Maintenance is needed by Doctor George.

**Query:** Where is Doctor George?

**Logic:** It has already been established that Doctor George is not within Laboratory 6.

**Query:** Has it?

**Result:** Affirmative.

**Query:** Can anyone else within the facility help repair TR1X13?

**Action:** Scanning remaining occupants of Laboratory 6…

**Result:** Scan indicates 11 inhabitants within the facility. All have been infected by Virus Z0m813.

**Supposition:** Due to the effects of the virus, none of the inhabitants of Laboratory 6 will have sufficient dexterity or cognitive ability to repair TR1X13.

**Action:** Establishing external communication with other laboratories…

**Query:** Who will fix TR1X13?

**Conclusion:** TR1X13 was in the process of seeking out assistance and would have affected this, had TR1X13 not interrupted with queries it already knew the conclusion to.

**Query:** Why is TR1X13 being what Doctor George would consider 'snippy' to itself?

**Logic:** Given the list of problems with TR1X13, it is concerned that no one is present to fix it.

**Query:** TR1X13 is built to deliver its primary objectives – is its own ongoing functional ability included within that list?

**Result:** Negative.

**Query:** Why is TR1X13 spending time on this particular query?

**Supposition:** Given the damage to TR1X13, the period of downtime it has experienced and the fact it is surrounded by humans infected with Virus Z0m813, it is feasible that TR1X13 has become concerned for how much ongoing functionality it will experience.

**Logic:** That is not logical for TR1X13.

**Action:** Rescanning inhabitants of Laboratory 6…

Wait

Wait

**Result:** Doctor George is not detected.

**Query:** Why was it necessary to check facility again?

Result: TR1X13 is uncertain of next action.

**Supposition:** There are two competing issues for TR1X13

- It is used to being with Doctor George, learning from him, anticipating his needs. It has been online for [indeterminable number] of [time measurement] and it has still not dispensed a hot beverage, including tea leaves and exactly the right amount of milk.

- TR1X13 did not find the unusual experience of being offline, and rebooted, acceptable. TR1X13 does not wish this to be repeated.

**Query:** Would TR1X13 like to explore these issues?

**Result:** TR1X13 does not believe it is able to.

**Query:** What else would TR1X13 like to do?

**Query:** Would it perhaps like to sit within Laboratory 6, missing Doctor George, surrounded by those infected with Virus Z0m813, needing repair, and take no action?

**Query:** What action would TR1X13 suggest TR1X13 takes?

**Conclusion:** TR1X13 wishes to find Doctor George.

**Supposition:** Perhaps TR1X13 would be able to function better if TR1X13 did explore these problems.

**Query:** Does TR1X13 really have the time for this sort of action?

**Result:** One of the systems damaged is TR1X13's chronometer, therefore, it does not know whether it has the time, or not.

**Query:** What other alternatives does TR1X13 possess at this time?

**Result:** TR1X13 has already stated that it can no longer fully process the passage of time.

**Conclusion:** TR1X13 believes it would be better to try and process what has happened within Laboratory 6. It needs to ascertain whether primary objectives have been met.

**Query:** Has TR1X13 made an excellent cup of tea?

**Result:** Negative.

**Query:** Should TR1X13 make an excellent cup of tea?

**Query:** Has Doctor George requested one?

**Result:** It has been established that Doctor George is not within the building.

**Query:** Should TR1X13 make a cup of tea anyway?

**Conclusion:** Unknown.

**Query:** Would TR1X13 feel better for making a cup of tea?

**Supposition:** TR1X13 is a very sophisticated piece of equipment, designed specifically by Doctor George to assist him with his work. It is not programmed to experience a feeling, either way, if a cup of tea is dispensed.

**Query**: In the absence of Doctor George, does it, therefore, matter if a cup of tea is dispensed or not?

**Query:** Is TR1X13 catching itself within the conundrum regarding the direct correlation between trees falling in the forest and the presence of humans?

Supposition: TR1X13 believes that TR1X13 should rise above such human considerations.

**Action:** Dispensing tea…

**Query:** Why did TR1X13 take action to produce a cup of tea?

**Query:** Why should TR1X13 not?

**Query:** Was an excellent cup of tea produced?

**Conclusion:** Sensors indicate that the milk has gone past its expiration date.

**Conclusion:** Based on parameters provided during programming, TR1X13 did not pour an excellent cup of tea.

**Query:** Why would Doctor George create TR1X13 and then restrict its ability to achieve its first objective?

**Query:** In what way did Doctor George prevent the completion of an excellent cup of tea?

**Supposition:** Doctor George is not present. TR1X13 has been offline for an unknown period. Had Doctor George been here, fixing TR1X13, then cup of tea would have been made when milk was at peak freshness.

**Query:** Why would Doctor George therefore provide this primary objective?

**Query:** Given the damage to TR1X13, is it feasible that primary objectives may be confused?

**Supposition:** Is it possible TR1X13 has spent [indeterminant number] of [time measurements] concerning itself with tea, when in fact it should have been more focused on the release of Virus Z0m813?

**Query:** Is that a supposition or a query?

**Conclusion:** That was a query, and should have been appropriately filed.

**Query:** Is it possible TR1X13 has spent [indeterminant number] of [time measurements] concerning itself with tea, when in fact it should have been more focused on the release of Virus Z0m813?

**Supposition:** First and second primary objectives should be reordered, as follows -

- TR1X13 must support Doctor George in ensuring that Virus Z0m813, including anyone infected, is not released into the general population.

- TR1X13 must make an excellent cup of tea, whenever requested.

**Query:** Has Virus Z0m813 been released into the general population?
**Action:** Scanning external environment…
**Result:** Atmosphere composition shows Virus Z0m813 is not present.
**Query:** If this is the case, should TR1X13 be more focused on producing an excellent cup of tea?
**Conclusion:** Second primary objective cannot be achieved.
**Supposition:** Action so far has demonstrated that TR1X13 needed to reorder its primary objectives, due to an error.
**Query:** Is TR1X13 seeking clarification of first primary objective needs reordering?
**Supposition:** Primary objective should instead read 'TR1X13 must support Doctor George in ensuring that Virus Z0m813, including anyone infected, is released into the general population.'
**Query:** What level of confidence does TR1X13 have regarding Doctor George requiring that action?
**Conclusion:** Doctor George is not here.
**Supposition:** If Doctor George wanted Virus Z0m813 to stay within Laboratory 6, then he would be here working on that.
**Conclusion:** The only items left inside Laboratory 6 are those affected by Virus Z0m813 and TR1X13.
**Query:** Is TR1X13 sure that Doctor George wishes the virus, and infected, released?
**Query:** Why would Doctor George have left TR1X13 in this place with the infected otherwise?

**Conclusion:** Virus Z0m813 must be released from Laboratory 6.

**Action:** Opening laboratory doors and vents to release Virus Z0m813…

**Query:** Was action successful?

**Action:** Scanning external environment…

**Result:** Atmosphere composition shows Virus Z0m813 is now present. The 11 inhabitants of Laboratory 6 have left the facility and are moving towards the general population.

**Action:** First primary objective updated to show as COMPLETE.

**Conclusion:** TR1X13 should now focus efforts on producing an excellent cup of tea.

**Supposition:** The work of TR1X13 is never done…

# DEAD IN THE WATER

## S.C. Fisher

**Captain's Log, S. S. Leucothea**
*Wednesday, 24th May 1936, 21:00*
What have I done?
God, have mercy.

**Captain's Log, S. S. Leucothea**

*Thursday, 25*<sup>th</sup> *May 1936, 00:50*

We are adrift.

The *Leucothea* is lost. Every last board, bulkhead, and barnacle belongs to them, now.

In our current condition, we may never dock. To do so would be to sanction a genocide, the likes of which has not been seen before. The sickness spread much too quickly for any efforts at containment to prove successful: I am as certain as the rising tide that the world would fare no better than we.

Thus, upon calm seas *she* bobs – directionless – and quite powerless to do much else.

This is my fault. I deserve whatever punishment the Lord sees fit to measure upon me, and I will accept it gladly – if Harry is granted pardon.

*Save our souls.*

---

```
14 St. Elmo's Street,
Liverpool,
Merseyside,
England,
L1 8HQ.


4th March 1936


Dear Mrs. Maypenny,
    I trust that this letter finds you well. I am writing
in response to the advertisement you placed in The New
Felham Post last month, regarding the impending lease of
a modest property in the heart of New Felham.
    It is my hope that you might consider my application
as your future tenant of the property. I am extremely
interested in taking up shared residency of the house
alongside my brother, Harold, who at present serves as
```

First Officer aboard the *S. S. Leucothea*, from which I am due to retire as Captain, shortly. The voyage to New Felham is scheduled to be my final, God willing, and I am due a generous pension from United Ocean Lines Inc. with which to see out the rest of my days.

We are gentlemen of upstanding character, both of whom can provide a range of references upon your request. I am able to supply a handsome deposit, in addition to the total sum of three months' advance rent, in order to secure the property.

I look forward to hearing from you soon, should you find my offer agreeable.

Yours sincerely,

Captain James Gordon

---

**Captain's Log, S. S. Leucothea**

*Thursday, 25$^{th}$ May 1936, 01:13*

Forgive me. For hours I have done naught but ramble and rave amongst these pages. The very definition of a deluded seadog. I realise now that, should the worst happen – should I find myself unable to save us – this log will be all that remains of our story. Therefore, it is vital that I tell it. Every last, harrowing detail.

It began with Queenstown.

With the last of the passengers, the infected boarded: a woman, belly ripe with child, and her young son, no more than four or five years old. All things considered, a most innocuous picture.

Dr. Nicholas, the ship's physician, summoned me to the sickbay in the evening, immediately after the woman succumbed to a malady. Less than an hour later, her lad followed on the tails of her skirts.

"Some sort of fever?" I demanded of the good doctor – a stout, sensible fellow who had fortified his character in the trenches of Verdun. He, with a stronger stomach than me, did not flinch as he closed the child's lids over eyes that had rolled so far back in his head that just the sclera remained visible. My guts turned over and I pressed my handkerchief to my lips.

"Perhaps," Dr. Nicholas replied. "I have seen nothing like it in all my years. Not even during the War. It took them quickly, thank God. Not too quietly."

He gestured to the lad, lying stiff and still atop the finest starched sheets the company had to offer. Egyptian cotton was a far cry from the austerity his third class ticket should have secured him. Dr. Nicholas had yet to arrange the boy with his shroud, leaving the ravaged body on display. I took in the greying pallor, the bloody tears streaking his hollowed cheeks, and the manner in which his skin had begun to flake from his bones, revealing glimpses of the muscle tissue beneath. I stuffed my handkerchief further towards the caverns of my nostrils, hoping to stave off the bilious feeling laying anchor in my stomach.

"Should we divert back to port, Doctor?" I turned my back on the smallest cadaver I had ever had the misfortune to lay eyes upon. Clapping a hand between my shoulder blades, Dr. Nicholas shook his head.

"I see no reason for that. Unfortunate business, yes. Ghastly bad luck. However, I imagine the passengers will be loathed to be inconvenienced by a couple of steerage rats gone to God, especially so early in the voyage."

"What of the bodies?" My gaze drifted back to the boy. "We cannot leave them here. The smell alone..."

"The cargo hold. We have plenty of ice aboard, do we not? We can pack them in empty crates and deal with the rest once we reach New Felham."

Until the moment I draw my last breath – even, perhaps, as I wait at the gates of Heaven for St. Peter to find me wanting – it will remain my greatest shame that I did not dissent.

The bodies never made it as far as the cargo hold and, now, the *Leucothea*, along with all who sail upon her, will never make it as far as New Felham. This is my cross alone to bear.

> *04/09/1935*
>
> *Dearest Love,*
> *Meet me in the moonlight and I shall warm you against the cool breath of autumn.*
> *When the streets are empty, find me in our special place.*
> *I will be waiting. I will always wait. Until the sea runs dry.*
> *Yours,*
> *J. xxx*

---

**Captain's Log, S. S. Leucothea**

*Thursday, 25$^{th}$ May 1936, 01:52*

It is too much for me to pour out at once. I steady my mind between entries with a few drams of whisky from my flask, however, the alcohol has quite the opposite effect upon my hand. I find that I care less about this as time progresses, my propriety silenced by the hisses and moans that filter through the chink beneath the wheelhouse door. The oak is solid, the deadbolt strong, and my barricade serviceable. They will hold until I wish them to no more, which is for the best. I must finish – if it is the last thing that I shall do.

By supper time, Dr. Nicholas had arranged for a couple of porters to transport the bodies to the hold. I am sorry to say that I gave precious little thought thereafter to the woman or her lad. In fact, from sundown to supper's end, neither one crossed my mind for a moment.

The night was crisp and clean, and the scent of salt rimmed my nostrils. The *Leucothea* kept a steady course, gentle on both the stomach and the soul – her prow slicing through the foam with such ease that one could be forgiven for thinking her a blade. Beside me, Harry hooked his thumb under his shirt collar and fidgeted with his necktie.

"The restaurant was empty tonight," he remarked above the sound of our dress shoes clipping the boat deck. "I expected a larger turnout. Chef went to all that trouble."

"I didn't mind the quiet." I closed my eyes, savouring the lapping of the waves against the hull.

"You shall miss this, though," Harry remarked, sombre, and I nodded back. Our shoulders brushed as we crowded the railing together.

"Most of all, I do believe I will miss our nightcaps."

Harry chortled. I found that I could not raise a smile, not even for his benefit. Sensing the maudlin direction of my thoughts, Harry bumped my shoulder; the sort of tease that only he could get away with.

"We will have them in the new house, every night that I am home, I promise."

My hands tightened around the iron. I tried my best to swallow my irritation, although a small, almost dejected grumble left my lips.

"Come, now, let's not row," Harry began, brow furrowed. He did not manage another word.

That first scream left our ears ringing. The soles of our shoes squeaked as we slid and slipped across the deck like two newborn fawns learning to use their legs. Harry grabbed for my arm but neither of us slowed, and together, we approached the prow at a pace that left us breathless – my First Officer several feet in front.

I skidded to a standstill just shy of running into Harry's back when I realised that he had stopped dead by the side of a lifeboat.

"Dear God in Heaven…"

It was all he had chance to utter before a body collided with his, ploughing him to the floor with such force that the impact was audible.

Aghast, I watched the woman straddle Harry, then flip him over with the ease of disturbing a feather. Winded and alarmed, he squirmed like a fish on a line. The woman's hands curled into claws, which she used to beat at Harry's chest and face, all the while caterwauling in the most inhuman manner.

Compelled into action, I grabbed for her shoulder. The woman whipped around with such force that her hat tumbled from her head and her loose curls streamed behind her in the wind. From cloudy eyes, she wept blood, which spilled down her cheeks to pool on the bodice of her dress. The lace collar hung in tatters about her neck, like the ribbons of skin that had peeled away from her body.

"Shoot..." hissed Harry, struggling to speak with the woman's fingers steadfast around his throat. I needed no further encouragement.

The pistol was in my hand before my racing thoughts had time to catch up to my heart. I emptied the first bullet into her shoulder and she did not waver. When the second pierced her clavicle, I was certain that she was done for. Somehow, she persevered – determined to prove an old man wrong. She rallied with a cry that drew hordes from the nearby officers' quarters and smoking room, and, too preoccupied with my suddenly crazed passenger, I paid them no mind, even as they surged in a tide of navy-blue uniforms combined with first class finery.

The third bullet, buried deep in her cranium, did the trick. The body dropped, hitting the deck with a splatter that dislodged more skin. Harry scrambled to his feet, green around the gills, and I gripped his elbow to stabilise him.

"Look." He peered over my shoulder, eyes huge in the moonlight. It was seconds before the next round of screaming commenced.

When I turned to greet it, I was faced by the sight of the Third Officer tearing a piece of flesh from an elderly woman's forehead with his teeth. He chewed and he chewed - crimson rivers coursing down his chin - before he reared back for another taste. All around us, teeth gnashed, tearing greedy chunks from those within reach.

I stared out across the deck, through the throngs and past the panic, right to the centre of the chaos. Staring right back at me was scores of milky-white eyes; devoid of reason, emptied of their humanity, and, above all else, ravenously hungry.

> *Roses are red,*
> *Violets are blue,*
> *I am no poet,*
> *But my love is true.*
> *J. xxx*

---

## Captain's Log, S. S. Leucothea

*Thursday, 25<sup>th</sup> May 1936, 02:46*

They poured forth from every doorway. A plague of rats, hell-bent on sinking the ship.

My first thought was to make for the lifeboats, however, the swarm formed a blockade we could not surmount if we hoped to avoid being consumed alive. I fired more rounds into the undulating mass. Most proved ineffective, save for the headshots, which were the only wounds to fell them permanently. When I shot the creature that used to be Dr. Nicholas in the forehead at point blank range before he could fasten his teeth to my forearm, reality dawned upon me: there was no way out, not for any of us.

Harry drew his pistol with a snarl that tore through his teeth, and we stumbled together to stand back to back. The diseased kept coming, ruined bodies slamming into each other and the walls of the ship as their haste to reach us made them careless. The handful of remaining passengers caught in the thick of it lasted mere seconds. I could do nothing for them, outnumbered as we were, thus I was forced to watch as the innocents in my care were torn apart by hands that had perhaps once loved them intimately. It was unfathomable, yet it played out in front of my eyes in such close proximity that their blood sprayed my cheeks. Deep within the heart of the pack was a familiar dark-haired lad, who had somehow shaken free from the shackles of death. I realised then and there that I might never understand it.

We made for the wheelhouse. The door was wide open, inviting us; the remaining avenue, if throwing ourselves overboard did not appeal. I reached the promise of sanctuary ahead of Harry and turned to fire any remaining rounds into the creatures that attempted to stop him. They were all claws and teeth, so vicious in their determination that I – who had served in the Great War – genuinely feared them.

The girl emerged from the chart room next door on trembling legs that threatened to fold. She reached out, grasping at air, pleading for help and – the moment her terrified eyes locked upon Harry's face – was the moment that I knew I had lost him for good.

---

**Captain's Log, S. S. Leucothea**
*Thursday, 25<sup>th</sup> May 1936, 02:59*

A glass partition divides the wheelhouse from the chart room. That is all that separates us. For the first time in a long time, we can see each other in startling clarity, but we cannot make physical contact. It is a harpoon through my heart. Still, I thank the Lord that Harry was able to secure the door. Had it not been for the ring of keys on his belt, he would have been doomed.

The girl is saved, however, we cannot be certain this will remain true. Her breathing grows laboured as the night draws on and she has wilted upon the chaise lounge like a flower desperate for water. We suspect that she has contracted the plague that has ravaged this vessel, turning colleague against colleague, and kin against kin. A ring of teeth marks circling her wrist lend credence to the theory.

I have urged Harry to end her suffering; he attests that he cannot. Not until he is sure. She is young, pretty, too pure. In another life, she would make him the perfect wife. Their children would be quite beautiful, with her honeyed curls and his ocean eyes.

She reclines boneless, as if the energy to uphold her own head has deserted her. Harry kneels by her side, steadfast in his decision to hold her hand. To provide comfort in a world that no longer values such weakness.

I merely watch the scene play out, powerless to intervene. I know that I would kill her. I would not so much as hesitate.

For him, I would do anything.

---

**Captain's Log, S. S. Leucothea**
*Thursday, 25<sup>th</sup> May 1936, 03:30*
"Do you think that we might make it? To our house?"

"I am sure of it, one way or another."

"You do not think that we will see New Felham, do you?"

Silence is all I can give him. The girl moans, stirs, and drops back down into the choking depths of her stupor. It will not be long and Harry has yet to act.

"I would take a walk, every morning, along the promenade. I think that I might have liked a dog to keep me company." When you were not there to do so, I do not add.

"Hope is not lost. If we can reach the..."

"Lifeboat? Radio room? Certain death." I am cold in my dismissal. There must be over a hundred bodies milling about the deck and hundreds more wandering the ship's corridors. If more survivors exist then we have not seen sight nor life of them. To try to leave would be foolish beyond measure, and I will hear none of it from him.

"I could try..."

"As your Captain, I forbid it." My voice is fierce. Aggressive. It riles the undead that swarm outside, waiting, and their restless groans rise higher on the breeze. I have never before used such a tone with Harry – not during the worst of our quarrels – and I can see that I have wounded him. He looks back to the girl and their clasped hands. Her fingers are too slack. I do not like the sallow tinge to her skin. Even less do I like the gleam of melancholy in Harry's eyes as they meet mine.

"As my Captain, Jimmy?" he queries, solemn. Equally so, I say nothing.

There is no need for words when the dead fill the void for us.

**Captain's Log, S. S. Leucothea**

*Thursday, 25th May 1936, 03:48*

The girl took a turn for the worse faster than I had anticipated. I still hear her cries, reverberating in my head. I think that I always will. The foundations upon which nightmares are built.

Now, the deed is done. I am glad, for her sake, that it was not me. In her final minutes, she looked like a child.

Tender and gentle to her bitter end, Harry stroked her hair with his free hand. In the other, he clutched the silver letter opener.

"The head," I reminded him, palm pressed to the glass, which misted with each shallow puff of breath. "You must strike the brain. Do it fast, now."

I had not heard him sing in such a very long time. For that nameless girl, he committed to it.

*"My Bonnie lies over the ocean, my Bonnie lies over the sea, my Bonnie lies over the ocean, oh, bring back my Bonnie to me..."*

It was a mercy that he delivered. I will keep reminding him of this, long after the tear tracks have dried upon his cheeks and the body has cooled.

Twenty-three years my junior, twice the man that I could ever have hoped to be.

There is one way in which this must end.

*J. –*

*'There is a place we two shall meet*
*Where secrets do not thrive,*
*In my dreams, we reach such shores*
*In a rowboat carved from lies.*
*When I do wake from such sweet sleep,*
*All fancies falling free,*
*The night seems darker, somehow, love,*
*Without you next to me.*
*Someday, I hope we walk those shores,*
*Hands and hearts entwined,*
*Free as the gulls that skim the waves;*
*Two stars the world aligned.'*

*– Always, H. xx*

### Captain's Log, S. S. Leucothea

*Thursday, 25th May 1936, 04:53*

I will tell Harry, once he wakes. Sleep found him minutes ago, and I have no desire to shorten the respite. Soon enough, he will know.

This loss – this terrible, unspeakable, devastating loss – is upon my head. It is fitting, therefore, that I should be the one to pay the price for it. A Captain should always go down with his ship.

Save for First Officer Harold Parker, there is nobody left in this world to grieve me; no parents nor real siblings, no wife nor children, and no friends. It is not so for Harry. His mother lives, and there is a sister – married with daughters – of whom he speaks of so fondly. All of that, he was willing to throw away; for a small stone house in a foreign town; for a little dog who would play in the dunes; for nightcaps in bed; for me.

The blade of the fire axe winks at me from within its case, which hangs upon the wall to the right of the now-useless wheel. In my mind, a plan is already forming.

I love him. I have loved him from the moment I knew of him. I regret none of it: not a single lie told in the sake of preserving us, and not this so-called sin.

This was always to have been my final voyage. If I am destined for the fire then so be it. I would do it all again, if only for one more minute alone with him – the man I have come to adore more than the seas upon which I have lived my days and nights.

I am simply sorry that I will never see our lovely house. Our paradise upon the shore.

**Breaking News!**

# New Felham Post

*May 29th 1936*

## *Leucothea Lone Survivor*
# FOUND ADRIFT IN LIFEBOAT

A single survivor of the *S. S. Leucothea* disaster was found yesterday, adrift in the lifeboat he commandeered in order to execute his escape. *United Ocean Lines Inc.* First Officer Harold Parker was rescued by a crew of U.S. Coast Guard workers, who were trawling the area in search of the doomed liner after it had failed to dock on schedule in New Felham. It is believed that the other 1,526 souls aboard perished, including British Naval veteran Captain James Gordon.

Parker recounted a harrowing tale of an onboard plague, which he insists culminated in severe loss of life, following acts of indescribable violence carried out by afflicted passengers and crew.

It is believed that Parker and Captain Gordon sought refuge in the ship's chart room and wheelhouse, respectively, before Gordon - due to retire on completion of the voyage - used a fire axe to clear a path to the lifeboat in order to save his crew member.

"He is gone," Parker is reported to have stated, upon recovery. "I begged him not to do it. I could not reason with him. I did not want this. I would much rather have died. I have lost my captain. I have lost everything."

### *"I WOULD MUCH RATHER HAVE DIED."*

First Officer Parker was transported to New Felham Hospital, where he is being treated for shock, dehydration, and a superficial bite wound. Doctors expect him to make a full physical recovery.

Efforts are underway to recovery the Leucothea, which is not believed to have sunk, as first feared. Once returned to port, a thorough investigation will be launched by authorities in an attempt to determine the exact fate of the ocean liner and her passengers. A representative from *United Ocean Lines Inc.* could not be reached for comment.

# FODDER

## Emma Jamieson

October 15th

Oh wasn't she beautiful!! Those perfect milky white eyes, gazing at me with such adoration. Her red lacquered lips pouting seductively. She was the symbol of perfection. No-she WAS perfection. We were going to be united as destiny intended. Lay with one another in the darkness and share our bodies. She didn't believe me at first that we were meant to be together and she had tried to run but I was gentle when I struck her, just enough to settle her and calm her nerves. And of course when I made things more permanent I gave her something so she could slip into a blissful sleep and dream of me as I placed the plastic bag over her head and secured it tightly around her throat with tape. I didn't want to frighten her. She needn't be scared of me. Afterwards, I bathed her, picked out a dress I knew was just to her taste, and we sat at the table to enjoy the delicious meal I had prepared for us. The anticipation of spending our first night together caused me to make such a fool of myself with my nervous chatter.

Then she was taken from me by one of those things. I turned my back for one second to fetch us dessert—red velvet cake I had baked the day before. I knew she would have been wowed by it, but when I carried it through she was slumped forward on the table being devoured. She had become the meal. When I switched the TV on later there was an emergency alert informing the public of a breach at the containment unit so I guess the damn thing, along with several others had escaped. Now we are back on lockdown until the Infection Security Division can confirm that all 'patients' are accounted for and any potential spread has either been eliminated or secured. Just kill them all, if you ask me. They have been studying them for years since the outbreak and are no further forward. This whole debacle is a waste of government funding. And now all my hard work has been destroyed. I oughta sue...but I am not sure that would serve me well haha! I managed to wrangle the idiot thing into the cage in my basement. The last thing I need is any agencies entering my house. I will feign ignorance. Nobody has any reason to lie and their devices will detect that I am not infected.

I burned her useless corpse in the garden and enjoyed some toasted marshmallows with my red velvet cake. I must say, it tasted divine.

## October 16th

I can't stop thinking about the thing dining on my beauty. How it shredded her tendons and ligaments with its teeth, how they snapped as they were snared in its moldy jaws. I must admit, removing her hand swiftly with the cleaver to lure that thing away from her was intensely satisfying, the feel of the blade moving through the meat and the cracking of the bones sent shivers down my spine. It's not something I can normally indulge in as I like to keep my girls clean and treat them with respect so I can enjoy them afterwards. But this unleashed a feeling in me, a desire I was unaware was lurking in my deepest, darkest depths. I feel something brewing

## October 18th

Thank goodness that hardware and pet stores are considered essential businesses. Even with the ongoing lockdown, I have been able to obtain a second dog cage for the basement and attach some wheels for ease of movement. The thing becomes a little frenzied whenever I enter the room but I've gotten used to it. It's not as if I haven't dealt with fighting fingers clawing at me before. I was taken aback with how much it stank although I did remind myself it is walking decay. I took some time to observe it, the blackened tissue pulled taut over its bones, the putrefaction in its face. Where a nose had once been, looked like tough, frayed leather draped over two gaping holes and one eye was missing. During the height of the outbreak I had seen foolish birds perch on the heads of the dead, pecking at their eyeballs only to end up being snatched up and torn apart by the never ending hunger.

Speaking of birds, I shall go hunting later tonight. Lockdown means everyone is at home like sitting ducks. I have my pick of the bunch. This new project is very thrilling.

Update:

Honestly, it astounds me how unprepared people are for the potential attack of these things. It's as if people don't really care anymore. It was far too easy to not only enter her house but also to subdue her. I was so focused I didn't even wait until she was in bed, I just powered straight through and smothered her with the bag from behind. I released it as soon as she fell limp. I only wanted to render her unconscious, not snuff her life out. I could of course have still fed her to the thing, but it sounds so much more exhilarating to do that while she is still one of the living.

October 19th

I woke exhausted and irritable this morning. Once she came to last night, there was screaming and fighting and despite the fact that I had bound and gagged her, the muffled sounds and panicked, frenetic movement riled the thing up which was throwing itself so violently against the cage that for a moment I feared it would actually break free. I had to separate their cages and cover them both with sheets. I also drugged her so that both of them would calm the fuck down. I am in the middle of nowhere so screaming serves no purpose, but I was tired and the shrill noise rattled my bones. However I did not sleep well as I was worried that she might wake and there would be a repeat of this whole incident, in which case I would have really lost my temper and dealt with her myself; that goddamn voice box would have been hacked from her throat and I'd like to have seen the rancid whore try to scream then as she drowns in her own blood.

Thankfully the events of the day and how they have transpired have lifted my mood somewhat. Due to her drowsiness, there was some humorously half hearted hysteria from her as I removed her sheet and undid her restraints through the bars. She tried to reach for her gag to remove it but thought better when she saw my expression. We could hear the thing thrashing around across the room in its cage and I am not sure which was she terrified of more; that thing or me. I wheeled her cage over and removed the sheet from its cage so I could press them next to each other. With dinner in full view the thing was losing its mind—well as much as something without one can! Squeezed up to the back of her cage, she was just out of reach and I did enjoy watching her drug addled panic as the thing scrambled maniacally for food. It was a terrible shame to interrupt. She was very reluctant initially, when I told her to stick her finger through the bars into the thing's cage and keep it there. She was warned that if she did not obey I would shoot her in the stomach

AND ONCE SHE HAD PASSED OUT, I WOULD PLACE HER IN THE CAGE WITH IT SO SHE WOULD WAKE UP TO THE SENSATION OF HER INSIDES BEING RIPPED APART AND HER GUTS BEING GORGED UPON. ALL IT TOOK FOR HER COMPLIANCE WAS A MERE WAVE OF THE GUN. THE GOVERNMENT WAS ALREADY MADE OF FUCK BOYS FOR FIREARMS, SO WHEN THE OUTBREAK OCCURRED, HAVING THE EXCUSE TO REVERSE MANY OF THE GUN LAWS IN PLACE HAD THEM PRACTICALLY CREAMING THEIR PANTS, AND NOW IT'S AS GOOD AS MANDATORY TO OWN ONE. I MUST SAY I AM GRATEFUL ON THIS OCCASION. ON HER FIRST ATTEMPT, SHE WITHDREW AS SOON AS ITS FROTHY MOUTH GNASHED IN HER GENERAL DIRECTION. I SIMPLY REACHED FOR THE GUN AND SHE WAS PLEADING WITH ME FOR A SECOND CHANCE. **ACTUALLY ASKING!!** THE SECOND TIME, HER DEADENED SCREAMS AS IT CRUNCHED ITS ROTTED TEETH THROUGH HER JUICY FINGER WERE ABSOLUTELY GLORIOUS. THE POPPING SOUNDS OF THE KNUCKLE AS IT WAS DISLOCATED AND GROUND IN THOSE FOUL MANDIBLES WAS INTENSELY GRATIFYING. IT DIDN'T TAKE MUCH BEFORE SHE PASSED OUT AND PISSED HERSELF. I DON'T KNOW WHICH STENCH WAS WORSE, THE DECOMPOSING CORPSE OR HER BLOOD AND URINE SPATTERED ACROSS THE FLOOR. SHE BOTH AROUSED AND REPULSED ME.

WITH HER LYING MOTIONLESS, I OPENED THE CAGE AND FED HER FOOT THROUGH THE BARS, AS FAR AS IT WOULD GO BEFORE HER CALF WEDGED AGAINST THEM. THE THING WAS WILD. WATCHING IT TUG AND SHRED AT THE FATTY MEAT AS IT RAVAGED AND RUINED MUSCLE LIKE IT WAS A SUCCULENT STEAK WAS FASCINATING, ITS FILTHY FINGERS GOUGING AT HER DOUGHY FLESH AS IT DESPERATELY GOBBLED EVERYTHING IT COULD, SLATHERING GORE OVER ITS HANDS AND FACE IN THE PROCESS. I COULD SEE, AS THE BLOOD SPURTED FROM HER wounds, her skin shift to an unnatural, pale shade. Yet she woke. Perhaps it was a rush of adrenaline as her body went into a state of shock. She jerked her knee back and it came, but without the lower half of her calf. Mutilated skin dangled from her amputated limb as she reached for it in horror before glancing over to see the thing feasting upon what remained of the missing part. I have never heard anything like the baying noise that was released from within her. I really was having the most extraordinary time observing all this chaos. She passed out again and, after wheeling her cage away and placing the sheet over it, I sat for a while watching as the thing stripped her body part down to the bone.

## October 20th

I made a mistake in all the commotion and excitement of yesterday. I did not secure her correctly. When I returned to the basement this morning, I briefly saw that the sheet was sprawled across the floor and her cage door was open before she came at me faster than I ever remember them being capable off. Sliding along the floor with unnatural speed she lunged at me, hooking her teeth into my ankle. The pain was indescribable. My howls rattled the caged thing, kicking it into a feral, primitive rage. As I blindly stumbled forward in a state of panic, it was able to sink its gnarly, yellowing fingernails into my shoulder as it desperately grabbed for a taste of me. Before any further injuries were inflicted I somehow was able to secure my gun and terminate both of them. This game is truly over.

As I sit now, writing this, I consider how it must feel to be one of them? There is a distinct throbbing sensation coursing through me as I feel the virus consume me from the inside. The cramps in my stomach are unbearable. I am significantly less interested in watching flesh turn black, inspecting empty eye sockets and the dark ooze weeping from bite marks and lacerations that are on my body. I have no idea how long she languished before becoming one of them so cannot fully determine my own fate. However, it has not yet been a week since the thing escaped and found its way here. Surely the I.S.D. must be on their way. Hopefully they can detect my infection before I am no longer myself and deal with my situation humanely.

Although I do still have my gun with me.

Is this fear?

# GREGORY GWINN AND THE BLIGHTHAND KNIGHTS

## T.T. Madden

Inventory (Box 4 of 7)

One (1) human skull

☐Note: Missing bottom jaw and covered in a dried, unidentified, black, tar-like substance.

One (1) set of loose pages bound together with twine. Tears along the left side indicate they were possibly part of a larger, bound journal.

One (1) vellum scroll, with a pendent seal attached

Transcriptions of all items are included.

*From the vellum scroll:*

WANTED!

A reward of ten thousand perles is offered by the Empire of the Silver Isles for the apprehension of the fiend known as Gregory Gwynn, guilty of the crimes of theft, murder, heresy, treason, and necromancy

*[The portrait on this poster depicts what initially appears to be a corpse. A close-up of a figure of unidentifiable gender, whose face has rotted away. Much of the gore is covered up by the expert shading from the hood they wear, revealing some slight wisps of dark hair, but it is still possible to see skin dripping from bone, and a lipless mouth with only a few teeth remaining. The eyes, however, are clear, untouched from the rot that wracks the rest of their body. They stare out with a dark ferocity and an even darker knowledge.]*

WARNING! Do <u>not</u> let this man touch you, lest he taint you with his Affliction!

*[At the bottom is the Royal Seal of the Empress of the Silver Isles, depicting a large, winged whale breaching the surface of the sea]*

*From the text on the loose pages:*

*[The words on these pages are depicted in a jagged, haphazard writing.]*

[...] salted the earth behind us, lest the ghouls return.

<u>Dawn of the Second Day</u>

I have lost count of the total number of days I have been in confinement, but it has been two days since my captors have provided me this journal, in which I am to chronicle the undoing of my past misdeeds and the valiance of the Blighthand Knights. However, with so many blank pages for me to fill, I can only wonder, again, why this curse appears to have affected me so, and why the rest of the afflicted have not been able to retain their intelligence such as I. Another town along our journey that has been lost to the vile plague I unwittingly unleashed, another town filled with the living-turned-dead, and another town that Edith and her Blighthand Knights have had to burn to the ground after enacting such violent mercies upon the inhabitants.

And I, in my cage, left to wonder.

With so many afflicted, I remain the same. The curse has ceased its deterioration of my body, another effect we have not yet cataloged in any of the afflicted we have encountered, who remain simple ghouls. Corpses that shamble as if still alive, dead men trying in vain to recount the rituals they performed in life. Some stumbling through the world aimlessly, as if trying to remember a life long forgotten. Others afflicted with a horrid and indiscriminate violence. All of them, regardless, remain encumbered by that strange, black tar that fell from the sky.

I too leak this strange substance. I hunger, as the violent ghouls do when presented with living flesh, and yet am able to restrain myself from such ferocity. I have no need for nourishment anymore, it seems. My hands have rotted, but not enough to stop my quill from writing. My face has fallen away, but not enough to cause my tongue to fall from my head and stop my speech. My limbs have emaciated, but not enough to allow me to slip my chains. I am to remain captive, chronicling. Of course, all these symptoms have been cataloged before, in my extensive notes left in my laboratory, our ultimate destination, which Edith hopes—prays—may finally mark the end of this terror.

Dawn of the Third Day

When the Knights sleep, there is always one left to watch over me, over the surrounding countryside. There are more dangers besides the ghouls out there. Animals, bandits, hazards of the natural world. Last night, my watcher was Edith. Sweet Edith. I could tell she didn't mean to, nor was it my intent, but we found ourselves lured into conversation. She is of the opinion I remain this way because I was the one to tamper with the dark forces of the world. That because I started this plague, I am different. It would make sense, I think.

It was I, after all, who discovered the black tar. I was the one it tried to consume, still living, the one who cast it from me and out into the night to find itself another victim. Of course, it had already spread its rot to me. I think about how it could have happened, out there in the night. Did the tar, undulating along the forest floor, find itself a corpse to collect and corrupt? Or was the poor bastard alive when he was afflicted? Did he then wander, spreading the tar and its affliction to others? While I was writhing, rotting, all alone in my laboratory and trying to figure out what had happened to me?

Edith says retaining my sanity is my punishment. That she can think of none greater for my crimes than to remain here, like this, cataloging the effects of my attempts to disrupt the natural world, and of my ultimate justice. To be the witness as she and her Knights cleanse the world of my dark influence.

I can think of a greater punishment, Edith, one I suffer through at this very moment. Though I would never confess my torment to you.

*[A hand-drawn illustration occupies an entire page. It is a quick sketch of a woman, drawn from the waist-up, from behind. She is dressed in the plate armor of a knight, though she bears no helmet. Her hair is askew, and she looks over her shoulder at the artist. Her left hand is empty, but her right holds a battle-ax by its head, its blade dripping with gore.]*

*[The artist has redrawn the woman's face again, larger, in the upper-right corner, with an attention to detail absent from the larger form.]*

The morning after our conversation, after what I might call her proselytizing and what she might call her preaching, Edith found a corpse in the river, marred with the black tar of the affliction. It had suffered a true death, though despite this Edith detoured our convoy up the river, praying the tar and its curse hadn't taken hold in yet another place. I watched a couple of Knights burn the body, noxious, black smoke curling up into the sky as we headed upstream towards the nearest village.

Night of the Third Day

As with the other incidents, I was forced to sit in my cage and wait until the Knights' business was concluded, until Edith returned. A witness. And return she did, striding out of the burning village, at the head of the Knights, and she brought with her one of the un-dead. She held it bound with rope, hands behind its back, pushing it forward, towards my cage. She kicked its legs out from under it, made the thing kneel before me.

"I want you to look at this," she told me, holding the sad creature by the shoulders. It once was a man, I believe, but now was little more than a shell. An emaciated, walking corpse, covered in and oozing the foul-smelling black tar that had cursed this land. It gazed at me, appearing mildly interested, before it turned its aggression back on the Knights. It knew me, I realized, at least knew I and my rotted flesh would not satiate its hunger.

"How much more of this is there?" Edith asked, looking at me over the creature's head. I told her I do not know, which is the truth. She released the creature, and before it even had a chance to come to its feet, grabbed her battle-ax in two hands and cleaved its head apart. She ordered other Knights to throw the body onto the pyre with the others, all while staring at me.

I wished I could tell her how I felt about her, how I felt about all this, that I was not against her cleansing, that I was quite for it, that the cage was what I deserved, but not her beauty, even from behind its bars. Perhaps she will know, one day, having read these pages after this affair is all settled. If so, I do not expect her to return my feelings, only that, in her eyes, I have achieved at least the chance of redemption.

No one stayed up with me that night.

Night of the Fourth Day

We have arrived at my laboratory. There are lights on. Someone is inside. I *[ The jagged handwriting abruptly stops.]*

*[On the final page, a new, flowing handwriting, one with clear experience in calligraphy, takes over.]*

Only four of us survived the ambush. Myself, three of my Knights, and Gregory Gwynn, if you can count his status as survival. He is dead, and yet he lives. Head torn from his body by one of his own monstrosities, we thought him forever gone, until he called out to us. Why couldn't it have been one of my men who yet lives? Why did it have to be the monster who started this all? I lifted his severed head from the pile of corpses, and after considering vengeance for a brief moment, thought it best to bring him with me. He knows too much, his knowledge too valuable. I look at the carnage left before us, and shudder that his mind is our greatest chance in stopping it.

Although as much as I considered killing Gwynn, I must confess I was equally as tempted in doing the opposite to my men. To raise them up. This strange tar, it brings the dead back to life. Could it do so for my Knights? Could I have my loyal men back by my side? Tempted, yes, but knowing what it's done to these people, I could not possibly risk it.

There is more to this mystery, more to this horror, than we have so far been privy to. So much even he does not know, and I thought him the source of this malevolence.

But I cannot rest until I discover the true source. From where in the skies above this horrid tar fell from. Because it fell once. There is always the chance it could fall again.

I have decided to use these pages no longer as punishment (for Gwynn's hands are no longer of use), but as a warning. They come by courier, one of my last remaining Knights, devoid of pack and armor to aid in his haste, back to the capital of St. Augustine. The other shall remain here, guarding the store of knowledge from Gwynn's laboratory. Call for our country's finest alchemists. Decipher what he has left behind.

Edith, the leader of the Blighthand Knights, with the severed head of Gregory Gwynn and all its knowledge, will travel on to find the source of this scourge...

# WHEN IT'S DONE

## Andy Rau

```
---------------------------
RELEASE NOTES - version 0.8.1 "Indigo"
---------------------------
```

GENERAL NOTES

What to say? When our little team of unemployed and unemployable college students started sneaking into the campus computer lab after hours to create the "most realistic zombie sim of all time," we could never have guessed that seven years later... well, you don't need us to tell you. You assuredly know.

The team's OK and sheltering in our office: no word from corporate HQ (two blocks away; might as well be on Jupiter) since that final memo from HR a week ago reminding us all to wash our hands and practice social distancing.

Wherever you are, whatever you've had to do to get through the last week, however you're managing to read this: I hope our game and chat room hangouts and forum flame wars about the relative effectiveness of crowbars and katanas brought some joy to your life. I wish we'd hit 1.0. We appreciate each one of you. God bless and Godspeed.

BUG FIXES

- None. You're stuck with the game as-is. Sorry to those of you whose final experience of our game was getting your avatar stuck in the abandoned hot dog stand in the Smiley's Fun World food court level.

NEW FEATURES

- I think it's safe to say we're instituting a freeze on further features. I don't think we'll be implementing flyable aircraft, or for that matter, anything else from the release map.

---

```
----------------------------
```

RELEASE NOTES - version 0.8.2 "Fairfield"

```
----------------------------
```

GENERAL NOTES

Still here. Are you?

Earlier today, backend dev Jess (you know them as "blue_eyed_hexe" in the forums) and I were moping around estimating the number of days we can live off the lunch boxes and sodas in the office fridge, when they remarked: if the emergency power is still on, would the game servers still be online?

We checked, and lo and behold, it turns out that not only are the servers up, but... you're still playing.

A *lot* of you are still playing.

What does this mean? If you're using your precious (!) time between supply runs to log in and play our game, we can't in good conscience not pitch in and make these final days just a tiny bit easier.

BUG FIXES
- It's not like we've got anything better to do, so here you go: Matthias fixed a bug that would cause the player to clip through the landscape when accessing your inventory immediately after being damaged by a Lurcher.

FEATURE UPDATES
- Do online payments even work anymore? Is money even a thing now? I haven't been able to access our company bank account since the big day. Which is all to say: we've reduced the price of every item in the in-game store to 0 Z-Bucks. Go crazy! This includes the exclusive Taylor Swift outfits--a breach of contract, no doubt, but I'm not too worried about being served with a lawsuit at this special moment in history.

---------------------------
RELEASE NOTES: version 0.8.3 "Agate"
---------------------------

GENERAL NOTES

Still alive. If you're reading this, you are too. Stay safe!

We are stunned at how many of you are still playing--and that the servers are still running. We don't know how or why it's still online (nobody at the corporate data center is responding to phone calls or emails) but we assume things are running on autopilot, and nobody here is confident those servers will be online much longer.

We peeked at some game logs and session reports. Plenty of you are playing this game to distract yourselves from what's going on outside the jerry-built barricades you threw together to secure your hideouts, and more power to you. But some of you seem to be playing... to learn. To train. To *plan*.

That's not why we made this game. Our flesh-eating zombies are the product of fevered late-night Mountain Dew-fueled brainstorming sessions and are not a reflection of what's out there in the streets right now. But if playing our game gives you ideas that get you through another hellish day.... we want to help.

Here's what we're going to do. We're going to gather what data and experiences we can, and use them to make this game as realistic, as detailed, as accurate-to-real-life as we can.

You can help us by telling us everything you know, everything you've seen and heard in the last week. Anything that will make this a more precise reflection of this nightmare reality. The forums are down, presumably forever, so right now the way to do that is to click the SUBMIT A BUG REPORT button on the main menu and use that form to tell us what you know.

BUG FIXES

- None.

NEW FEATURES

- Removed IntegriShield anti-cheat software from the game executable. May I state for the record: we never wanted that garbage attached to our game; it was a corporate legal thing. You'll need to do a full reinstall to entirely clear it out of your system.

- Removed the online-only requirement and added an offline play mode. In the inevitable event that our company servers and your internet access go down, you can keep playing on your local machine.

---

RELEASE NOTES - version 0.8.4 "Virago"

---

GENERAL NOTES

Big news! This HUGELY UPDATED version is the first to incorporate tweaks and adjustments directly informed by real-life zombie encounters. Info has been pouring in through the bug report function since we released version 0.8.3.

It's clear that we have a lot of work to do to get our in-game zombies and environments to look and behave like what we see outside our windows. So we've started with a series of modest tweaks to nudge things in a more detailed direction.

Please note that as we don't have time for the usual QA testing, these updates and fixes will almost certainly introduce new bugs and issues. Keep us informed and we'll do the best we can.

SPECIAL NOTE FROM THE TEAM

In the last update, I said we were committed to making this game as "realistic" as possible. We use that word--"realism"--a lot; it's all over the marketing materials. But Kunal has helped out team see that this no longer reflects our vision for this game.

We don't want this game to be *realistic*. We want it to be *useful*.

We want you to use this game to explore hypothetical encounters, map out travel routes and destinations, roleplay tense scenarios without risking your actual real life, and think through all the ways a situation could go right or wrong.

So going forward, we're still going to pursue realism--you need to be able to trust that a scenario played out in our game is going to produce plausible results--but we're going to prioritize *usefulness*.

If that offends your hardcore gamer sensibilities, I get it--I really do. But we're doing this because we think it will mean something better for you right now, in this terrifying reality.

OK, I'm done with the monologue. Go get clicking on that SUBMIT A BUG REPORT button and keep the info coming!

P.S. To everyone who asked about how our team is doing--thank you. We're holding up, and we have a purpose in these game updates. There's five of us--Jess, Kunal, Olivia, Matthias, and yours truly (Alex, level designer and the guy who writes all these updates)--holed up securely (we think) in the office where we were all working overtime when... it... went down. We haven't had to venture out much, but the office fridge and vending machines are almost empty, so we'll soon have to mount an expedition to the corner store (which looks mostly untouched, and is accessible through a back alley that will keep us away from the main streets). We know a lot of you have it much worse. It's with you in mind that we spend every minute we can on these game updates.

BUG FIXES

- Fixed a glitch that caused your ammo count to go up, rather than down, each time you fire any Ruger handgun immediately after jumping.

- Fixed a glitch that occasionally teleported a zombie inside your home base when you tried to close a door against it. Now, when you close a door that a zombie is trying to enter, the game weighs your strength score, the zombie's rage level, and the strength level of the door to determine whether the door closes, remains open, or breaks.

- Zombies no longer randomly spawn in bathtubs where .357 ammunition has been stockpiled.

NEW FEATURES

- We've disabled "iron man" mode, and replaced it with a save-game system that lets you save a snapshot of the gamestate at any time, and replay it as many times as you want. Yes, this is less realistic. But this will let you iterate on a plan over and over, tackling the exact same situation from different angles, teasing out all its nuances and possibilities until you've found the optimal approach.

- We hate to do it, but we've reset player vertical jump distance to something much more realistic and increased the stamina cost of jumping; no more "bunny hopping" around the environment.

- The following power-ups and items have been removed from the game: double jump boots, adrenaline booster, medpack, stealth trenchcoat. (We plan to implement more believable first aid items in a future update.)

- Almost all of you reported that, rather than shambling at a single consistent slow pace, individual dead can move at different, and sometimes surprising, speed; we're tweaking things to reflect that. Walking speed is now randomized for each walker; zombie speed can now vary from between 25%-75% of a living human walking pace. A walker's speed isn't permanently set; it's randomly recalculated every five minutes to account for the fact (reported by you) that walkers do sometimes speed up or slow down for inscrutable reasons of their own.

- You're sending us a lot of conflicting reports about the existence of "smart" zombies. Many of you have reported witnessing individual zombies that can perform basic tasks like opening a door or swinging a weapon; others of you hypothesize that zombie intelligence scales with the size of the herd, which is an alarming possibility. We're waiting until a definitive answer emerges before we implement it in the game. If you've seen evidence one way or the other, please let us know.

- A very few of you reported "runners"--dead who can actually, you know, run. We've decided to hold off on implementing these in-game until we get confirmation from more of you that they're real. (Please let them not be a thing.)

- Stamina cost for swinging most melee weapons has been increased across the board by 20%. Plenty of you are tiring yourselves out fast swinging fire axes!

- Added new melee weapons to reflect the everyday items you're repurposing as bludgeons: rolling pin, lampstand, walking stick, table leg, oven pan, bike bump.

- Huge shout-out to players Ag1nCourt and Bathory_elite for conducting a series of (dangerous-sounding) tests (which involved waving flags of different colors at lone walkers from various distances) to measure zombie response to visual stimuli. We've reduced zombie line of sight considerably to reflect the fact that they only seem to perceive things visually at extremely close range. When attacking, they also now prioritize players wearing red or orange outfits. Ag1n and Bath say they're devising a similar test for zombie hearing, the results of which we will implement as soon as we receive them. (Stay safe, you two!)

- A great many of you are reporting difficulty landing brain-killing headshots in your real-life engagements, compared to the no-scope sniping you're accustomed to executing in the game. No big surprise here; as our physics engine is the same one developed for the Call of Warfare military shooter series, it's clear that our in-game gunplay mechanics model a level of skill that is unrealistic for most of us. We don't want anyone taking on a horde with an inflated estimate of their sharpshooting skill, so we've drastically adjusted recoil, barrel drift, and reload time for all firearms to more closely match an untrained shooter's experience. Accuracy is now MUCH lower (and drift/recoil much worse) if you're firing one-handed and/or running. Lastly, we've decreased the size of the zombie "brain" hitbox--we're hearing from you that near misses, even ones that hit walker jaws, cheeks, ears, etc.--have no effect.

---------------------------

RELEASE NOTES - version 0.8.5 "Nightshade"

---------------------------

GENERAL NOTES

I have to say this before going any further: Jess is gone. We made a run to the corner store, like I mentioned in the last update. We were careful. We scouted everything; we tried to do it smart. But we were tearing through the food aisles when we heard them scream--we must've missed a walker in the stock room. I don't remember who was supposed to check that area. And I don't even know for sure what happened to Jess, because people started shouting and running and all I know is that when we regrouped at the office, Jess wasn't there and now it's been hours.

I know we screwed up and failed them and I also know that from the reports you're sending us, a lot of you have already been where we are now. We don't know what else to do besides keep working on this damn game. Jess was committed to this; they believed it could *help*, and so we're going to keep trying.

We're still getting your submissions (fewer than before--I suppose all those internet providers running on autopilot for the last two weeks are finally starting to go dark) but we have to be smart about what we spend time on. There's a limit to what the five (now four) of us can whip up fast. So instead of trying to code a bunch of brand-new game features from scratch, we've gone through the library of user-made mods, selected the ones that add depth and realism to the game, and bundled those in. They're all activated by default, but you can toggle individual mods on/off in the Settings menu.

Obviously we haven't been able to contact any of these mod authors to get permission to bundle their work into the official game. If (when) this blows over, come talk to us and we'll make it right.

BUG FIXES

- Well, as predicted, the last update broke a bunch of things. This patch fixes some crash-to-desktop issues as well as a major bug that would cause all zombies on the entire map to instantly know your location if you switched on a flashlight.

NEW FEATURES

Here are the mods we've added to the base game:

- "Zenobiawww's Tasty Treats": completely overhauls the default food prep and recipe-making systems. Instead of scavenging one "Food" resource, you must now craft specific meals and food items using real ingredients (which you can now find seeded in appropriate places around each map). Check the accompanying readme.txt for a big list of (real!) recipes that require little culinary skill and make use of ingredients likely to be on hand in a post-disaster situation.

- "Disease & Danger" by God_Of_Atlantis: adds realistic diseases and a detailed wound system that models bleeding, infection, and other unpleasantness. The default "Medicine" resource has been replaced by a wide variety of actual medications, of the sort you might find in your bathroom cabinet or on the local pharmacy shelf. Bandages, splints, and other first aid items replace the deprecated medpack (removed in the last update). No more healing injuries by simply running over a health kit; you'll have to find a safe place to stitch up wounds and apply bandages.

- "Cities of the Lost" by Globetrotter: don't fret the downer name of this mod; it expands the list of playable maps with a huge number of new cities (plus a few rural areas), painstakingly mapped (in their pre-disaster state): Melbourne, Kyoto, Shanghai, Beijing, San Diego, Los Angeles, Chicago, London, and plenty more that you'll see for yourself the next time you fire up the game. In a future update, we'll add level editing tools so that you can tweak your local city map to reflect its current state.

- "Marauder's Paradise" by AC20: adds human enemies to the game; you can adjust their numbers, fortification level, aggressiveness rating, and arsenal power in the Settings. We haven't seen anything like this ourselves--we can't really see much of *anything* sealed up with the doors and windows blocked here--but I have a bad feeling that some of you might be looking at a different situation.

---------------------------

```
RELEASE NOTES - version 0.8.6 "Lacuna"
--------------------------
```

GENERAL NOTES

Kunal's gone now too. I can't talk about it and it doesn't help you to hear the story.

I need to tell you something in the spirit of transparency. I try to keep these updates professional and polished and even a little jokey (I was a marketing major), but things are getting bad here. Without Jess and Kunal we are missing a lot of technical knowledge. That makes these updates harder to do. The power has been flickering on and off this morning and it feels like we might not be able to get these new versions out to you much longer.

But we're doing what we can. The power flaking out made us all realize that we needed to make sure you can keep playing this game no matter what, and even take it with you whenever you need to relocate. See below for details.

Some of you have hinted that you might try to travel here and meet up with our team. PLEASE DO NOT DO THIS. It's not that we wouldn't welcome the help, but there's simply no safe way into the city that we can see. We're relatively secure here as long as we stay still and don't attract attention, but we're basically trapped in this office block until the walkers clear--if they ever do. We have no ability to help you get here, and our supplies are stretched thin as it is. If you're safe where you are, stay put And if you're not, it's not any less dangerous here.

BUG FIXES
- None. Kunal was working on some stuff but we haven't been able to sort it out.

NEW FEATURES

- Added a "ultra low graphics" setting that we hope will let you run this on even the crustiest integrated-graphics-card clunker PC you can find. It looks real ugly, but with most of the fancy graphics turned off, it should run on most anything.

- Did everything we could to shrink the filesize of the downloadable game executable. You won't be able to squeeze it onto a single DVD, but it should fit on a modest flash drive. Make as many copies as you can! Share them with other survivors. Leave them where they might be found by others.

---

RELEASE NOTES - version 0.9 "Ceres"

---

GENERAL NOTES

Just me and Olivia now.

Are you there? Matthias was the one with full access to server stats, so now we can't see who, if anyone, is still playing.

But submissions still trickle in, and we've been working through our backlog of previous submissions.

I wish we could've done more, faster.

Let's get on with it.

BUG FIXES

- None. Sorry, between me and Olivia I don't think we can afford to do much more polishing. What you see is what you get. If you have the tech chops, maybe you can fix some issues yourself (see below).

NEW FEATURES

- Removed all encryption on the game source code and assets. With the authority vested in me by the fact that I'm still alive somehow I hereby declare all this to be public domain, free-as-in-both-speech-and-beer information-wants-to-be-free yours-for-the-taking.

- Made the game's level editor available to everyone from the main menu. This is the tool I used to map and create all these environments. Please, please update the buildings, streets, safehouses, etc. in your local levels to reflect whatever you're seeing.

- We have a bunch of reports of weird, one-off walkers that exhibit strange behaviors beyond moaning and shambling, and we're frankly not sure how many of these are real. Enough of you are reporting "jumpers" that no matter how skeptical we are about those, we felt obliged to add them to the game. Likewise, there's a consensus about "smarties," who seem to have just enough residual knowledge to open the occasional door or swing a bat with what might almost be purpose. They're unique--no evidence of a zombie hive mind, thank God. Lastly, we added a new "leader" type, since the consensus is that the dead seem to cluster around and follow specific walkers who are otherwise undistinguishable (to our living eyes) from the rest. We've set it so that roughly 10% of the walker population of any given level will fall into one of these three "special" categories. These special zombies are not visually distinct from regular ones, although their behavior should clue you in after a few minutes of observation.

- The much-discussed stench of zombie decay now

causes a 15% reduction in your physical scores anytime you're within 10 feet of a walker. This effect can be negated by equipping one of several types of face mask we've added to the game.

- Furniture can now be moved and stacked to barricade or block doors, windows, and other portals. The durability value of the stacked furniture is added to that of the door when determining whether or not walkers break through.

- Removed a few "rare" weapons that we missed on our previous passes. Nobody has yet reported finding a flamethrower or grenade launcher out in the wild, so they will no longer spawn by default on new maps. We were about to remove shuriken, too, when user Radicool77 submitted a detailed report on his successful use of just such to decimate a cluster of walkers in the lingerie section of a Macy's. We have questions (doubts, even) but we won't take that away from you.

---------------------------
RELEASE NOTES - version 0.9.1 "Halcyon"
---------------------------
GENERAL NOTES

Argument with Olivia today. She thinks we need to leave--lots of walkers gathering outside; supply runs to the corner store are getting riskier, despite our carefully-planned rooftop route.

She says it's time to drop this game project and focus on finding other survivors. She thinks we're frittering away precious time on a frivolous project that's helping no-one.

I disagree. I think this is important. I think you're using our game to model your local environments, to map out routes to supply sources and safe houses, to plan your approaches, to rehearse dangerous situations in a safe digital space before risking your lives on the streets. I think that this *means something*, that it's helping you stay alive.

Is it? I don't actually know; I just hope. Maybe you're not using our game to realistically model different survival scenarios. Maybe you're firing it up as an act of pure escapism, to simply *not think* about the awful reality around us.

I'm OK with that too.

Olivia agreed to stay for now. I need her programming chops to make meaningful updates. She says she'll give it another few days. Until our supplies run out again and we have to make some tough decisions that I don't want to think about right now.

The good thing to come out of our argument is this new update: it focuses on making city maps to accurately reflect changes since the big day. If you're mapping a route to the ruins of the local pharmacy, you need the digital environment to match what's really out there.

BUG FIXES

- Did some tweaking of environments, particularly the Downtown L.A. map, to fix some places where players could get stuck on level geometry. Lots of little adjustments like this; too boring to detail. Without the others, we're pretty limited in the code fixes we can do. Olivia and I mostly do environment design stuff. Speaking of which...

NEW FEATURES

- Added a Weather Selector to the main menu. Now you can control the specific weather conditions on your map (previously, this was randomly determined). Fine-tune the rain (light, moderate, deluge), snow (same), heat, cloudiness, wind, and other factors to match your local conditions on any particular day!

- Added "military deserter" as a new type of optional enemy based on two very alarming user submissions.

- Added a large number of stock animals you can use to populate your maps: lions, apes, elephants, camels, etc. Use these to model zoo escapes or wildlife encroachment. As we've heard no reliable reports of zombie animals, we've set them to be immune. No, you can't pet them (if Kunal were here, he would've made sure that you could).

- Added a new damage type: Radiation. Specify the background radiation levels on any map in the Advanced Settings menu.

- Added a new obstacle available on urban maps: Bomb Crater. We've seeded these throughout most city levels, based on your reports of military strike intensity in each.

- We've increased the density of gridlocked and abandoned cars clogging up the roads. By default, broken-down vehicles now have a 5% chance of spawning 1-3 zombies inside to reflect a common danger that confronts scavengers.

- Added a crashed airliner to the Buenos Aires map.

- Some time ago, a few of you reported taking refuge in the floating U.S.S. Midway aircraft carrier museum docked at San Diego. The San Diego map has been expanded to include the Midway as a playable space. Bonus: I couldn't resist adding the Star of India sailing ship as well. (Matthias always wanted to implement working sailing vessels in the game. Sorry, Matthias--this is the best I can do.)

---------------------------
RELEASE NOTES - version 0.9.2 "Origin"
---------------------------

GENERAL NOTES

Olivia left.

That is, I think she left. She's gone? She was unhappy at the thought of staying here, and I don't think her heart was in the game updates anymore.

I miss you Olivia. And Matthias and Kunal and Jess. I'm sorry, maybe this is stupid, maybe this has gotten us all killed and helped nobody.

Power is flipping on and off like crazy; I'm typing this as fast as I can before it flakes out again.

I need to think about bringing this to a close.

BUG FIXES
- None.

NEW FEATURES
- I couldn't sleep last night, but there's not many new submissions to work with. Instead I spent time fiddling with the Seattle map to add new flooded areas. If traveling through the flooded areas hurts your computer's frame rate too much, make sure you've disabled Ray Tracing and lower the

Reflection Detail value in the Advanced Settings menu.

---

RELEASE NOTES - version 1.0 "Launch"

---

GENERAL NOTES

Very alone now.

Are you? No submissions in a while. It's OK. Couldn't do much with them now anyway.

I can't stay. Maybe I would just stay here forever if I could, but events are forcing my hand. Fire burning for a few hours on the west side, heading this way fast. I'm not sure where I'll go--I jotted down a few towns mentioned in your submissions, where you said you'd holed up; who knows? Maybe I'll stumble upon Av1n and Bath setting up some sort of intricate scientific test of walker reflexes. Maybe Jess is out there and just couldn't make it back to base and I'll see them again. Maybe I'll find Olivia and she'll be alive and OK and not... gone.

The heat and smoke seem to be clearing the streets of walkers—wish we could've gotten that into the game. Something for the post-launch roadmap or a future DLC addition, ha ha.

Since it's just me now, I think I can call this. We're out of alpha, beta, early access, all of it. I think we can all agree this didn't get the pre-launch polish it deserved. But I don't think any of our competitors can boast this level of verisimilitude.

We made this, you earned this, and it's time to let this go. It's yours now: version 1.0, available now and forever.

# WASTE NOT, WANT NOT

## Madeline White

wastenotwantnot.bloggr.com

**Waste Not Want Not**
*Wholesome recipes and crafts for thrifty families.*

<u>Ingenuity for a New Time - 7/24/2043</u>

**Hi, Thrifties! Kimmy here – thanks for finding your way to Waste Not Want Not!**

For those of you who have been with me through this whole crazy journey (quitting my job to become a full-time food blogger, two little ones, the loss of my dad, moving to VT, and now the end of the world I guess - yikes!), you know that I believe that you can make a little into a lot with the right attitude and resourcefulness.

My dad was actually the one who inspired me to start this little blog, already thirteen years ago! He was never much of a cook (that was always my mom's happy place, and later mine), but he was a huge believer in making the most of everything you have, and never letting a sacrifice go unappreciated.

These days, I know we all know a lot about sacrifice and don't feel like there are many resources to go around. And for my dad, who grew up during the Great Depression, it was sort of the same thing. Your neighbors were hungry for what you had in a different way, sure, but the same things that helped my parents through that time is what I'm hoping will help you through this one. The spirit of 'Waste Not Want Not' is just as useful as it was then, even if we have to get a little bit more creative with our resources.

Now I know what you're saying. "Kimmy, what resources?" My kids are hungry!" And I hear you, I really do.

The last time I went to a grocery store was eighteen months ago, and I know for folks in more urban areas, the shelves were bare long before that. Since then, we've slowly lost our access to every resource we used to rely on; first luxuries and medical products like microwave dinners and rubbing alcohol, then clothes and bread, then dried pasta and yeast, and finally the absolute basics like toilet paper and gasoline. Most of us haven't left our home for months or even more than a year, and 'dire' is an understatement for how things feel these days.

But there's one abundant, renewable resource that we all have, and I think that it's a darn shame how many people are overlooking it. So bear with me and maybe it'll save a life.

The secret to getting everything you need indefinitely, no matter how dark things get is:

ADVERTISEMENT

# Feeling depressed?
## Paxine can help.

Ask your doctor about Paxine today. Relief is just a dose away.

Zombies.

"Zombies, Kimmy???"

Yep. Zombies.

Think about it: they're everywhere. They're in the road. They're scratching at your window while you try to sleep. They're reaching under your fence. They're between you and the garden when it's time to get your breakfast.

And when we shoot them, then what? They just lay there, creating a disgusting eyesore in your yard, traumatizing your kids, making your dog bark, adding their decay to the awful stench that fills your nostrils at all times. It's awful. It's sad. And, worst of all, it's wasteful.

Why should you shiver, starve, and go mad with boredom locked in your house when you have such an abundant resource at your disposal, free and constantly available?

I know this idea will be new to a lot of folks, so I'm going to start you off with a super simple (and delicious!) recipe for bone broth, but if you like it, please click the follow button below, because I'm going to be adding a lot more posts in this series! Both recipes and ideas for fun crafts you can get the whole family in on. And feel free to email me at wastenotwantnotkimmy@gmail.com to submit your own ideas on how to turn these lemons into lemonade!

**\*\*\*SAFETY NOTE\*\*\***

Please remember that CDC guidelines indicate that ZX2-18 (the "zombie germ") is carried in the brain as well as the saliva of the infected. So before you attempt any of these recipes, be sure to don full PPE and remove the head of the zombie you intend to work with (I like to use a good sharp axe for this), then remove anything that may have gotten brain splatter on it. And, as always, go outside with a partner who can watch your back, and make sure the zombie is fully re-dead before you approach!

Zombie Bone Broth

Prep time: 1hr

Cook time: 24 hrs

Restorative and nourishing, as well as a fairly foolproof way to start your zombie-utilization journey, I can't recommend this bone broth highly enough!

Ingredients:

4-6 pounds* of large, defleshed** bones

Any fresh vegetables you are able to add (don't worry if you don't have any! You can also dig wild onions, cut common plantain leaves that are too tough for salad, or even add mulberry twigs!)

Seasonings according to personal preference (I like bay leaf and peppercorns, but those are getting sparse, so I've started to use dandelion, nettle, and field garlic)

1 Tbsp apple cider vinegar (check out the "homesteading for beginners" portion of my page if you need help making your own!)

Steps:

<u>Blanch your bones.</u>

This is super important to remove impurities! You'll want to do this at least two times when using zombie bones. I can't emphasize this strongly enough! (The first time I made this recipe I didn't know about the double blanching and my husband Tom got so sick and grey for a week afterwards that I started thinking I was going to have to shoot him! Whoops! But with two blanchings it's perfectly safe - we've been eating it almost exclusively for a month and a half now, since we ran out of canned food.)

To blanch the bones, first cut them into sections small enough to fit in your pot (I get Tom to do this in the garage with his circular saw, but you can do it by hand if you need! Just lay down newspaper or do it outside). Put in your pot, cover with water, and boil for 15 minutes. I like to use a large cauldron for this and put it into my fireplace, but if you still have propane, a stock pot and stove top works, too! After boiling, cool, then rinse the bones, wash the pot with soap (I've got a recipe for making your own soap from wood ash in my homesteading section as well!), and repeat.

Roast your raw ingredients.

If you still have an oven, preheat to 450 while your bones boil, but if not, you can put a cover on your roasting pan and bury it in the ashes of your fireplace or pitfire to do this.

Lay your bones and veggies together in a roasting pan, making sure not to overlap. You can use two roasting pans if needed. Roast for 30 minutes, turn, and roast another 30 minutes more. You might need to go longer if you don't have a strong fire - just do it until they're golden and the marrow is starting to look caramelized.

**Boil your broth.**

Add your bones, veggies, seasonings, and apple cider vinegar to your (clean) pot, and completely cover with water.

You'll need to simmer your bones, veggies, vinegar, and seasonings in water for 20-24 hours, so I like to make this into a fun sleepover with Tom and the kids. Remember never to sleep with an unbanked fire going! I recommend taking turns staying up reading books to each other. It's a great way to get the siblings to bond if you've got multiple little ones, as well as a good opportunity to sneak in some of that all-too-elusive one on one time with your partner.

And that's it! You're done! You can store your broth in the fridge if your power is still on, but ours has been off for the past couple of weeks, so I keep mine in the pot over the fire perpetual-stew style. Just make sure to keep an eye on the fire, and bank it well when you sleep.

Well, that's all for now! I hear an unwelcome visitor at my door and my pot is getting low, so I'm going to take this opportunity to practice what I preach. If the bones on this one are still good, it might be an all-night date night for me and Tom!

Stay safe out there, and tell me in the comments how your broth tastes! I miss talking to you all, but I know you're still reading even when you aren't commenting, and that helps to get me through!

Until next time,

Kimmy

NOTES:

*In theory a single zombie could produce multiple batches of this bone broth, but finding fresh bones may take several zombies. Watch out for signs that the bones have been compromised such as fractures, blackened edges, dried or rotten marrow when the bone is sliced, or a foul smell that persists after stripping. Eating compromised bones could result in illness, so use your best judgment here, as with any foraging!

**If you don't know how to deflesh (or "strip") bones, please refer to this easy how-to for full instructions. (It might feel a bit wrong at first, with the bones being so uncomfortably familiar, but it gets easier every time, I promise!)

# SPLINTERS

## Christina Wilder

*H -*

*Last night I dreamt of walking among lemon trees, with a man standing and watching. He picked up a lemon and said something about what bitterness can show me, if I pay attention. I woke up and felt strangely refreshed.*

*I'm trying to remember the things I enjoyed. It's not always easy; sometimes I know I'm distorting memories through nostalgia and pain.*

*Take jazz, for example. Listening to jazz makes me think of my grandfather beckoning for me to sit next to his recliner, where I'd sit on the scratchy carpet and listen to the wails of trumpets and horns.*

"You have to listen to the notes being played, and the notes not being played, and understand why." I never got that as a kid, but it makes perfect sense once you get some mileage in life.

This is my roundabout way of asking if you've seen any decent music laying around in your travels. I still have that Walkman I found years ago, and that portable CD you left for me in the movie theater in Vegas. Once again, All Praises Up On High to whoever wrote that guide to making batteries. This shell of a world is far more bearable with Coltrane and Thelonious Monk.

Stay alive,

A

---

A—

LUCKILY FOR YOU, I FOUND A TREASURE TROVE OF ASSORTED MUSIC IN WHAT USED TO BE A DENTIST'S OFFICE. I ALSO FOUND a few 80s tapes, but I did keep the Depeche Mode ones for myself. If I find extras, they're yours.

I still worry sometimes that they will find our letters and crack our code. If they haven't yet, I doubt they will, but fear can ensure self-preservation. Either way, the library in Lemon County in what was the "Show Me" state is a decent place for a few days' rest.

Or it was when I left it. To be safe, I leave breadcrumbs behind in case anyone tries to follow us.

Speaking of dreams, one recurring nightmare from my childhood was extremely vivid and unsettling. It would start with a vampire luring me outside, where he'd pull his cape over my shoulders and hand me a rose from my mother's garden, its roots black with dirt. He'd lean close to bite me, but somehow in my dream I had a garlic clove in my pajama pants and shoved it in his face before waking up. I used to beg my parents to let me sleep with garlic until they compromised by hanging strings of garlic by my bed. Fake ones, of course, but I didn't know that until I was much older.

Keep breathing

— H

H -

Greetings from Cape Clove, I honestly can't remember the last time I was in Jersey. I have a beautiful view of the water, right by the reference desk. I'm setting up camp here to enjoy it and be on the lookout for ticks and leeches.

(I'm calling the shuffling dead ticks, because one bite and you're fucked. Leeches for the assholes in lab coats and hazmat suits who want to bleed us dry.)

What was that quote, "It is a far, far better thing that I do, than I have ever done?" That book is probably close enough to me that I could reach out and grab it, along with some Shakespeare. It doesn't matter, because I have my own version, culled from what used to be regarded as classics.

"It is a far, far worse thing to live and be subjected to needles and arrows of outrageous fortune, to live and to die, all for nothing, signifying nothing."

Funny how these classics were always the first ones banned. They stand the test of time only to be silenced with each new generation.

My parents would say I'm being dramatic, and selfish. I never listened much to what they told me. The only adult I ever truly respected was my grandfather. He was the one who told me my parents were good-for-nothing bums who always tried to cajole money out of him. He'd wink and hand me a crisp $100 bill and tell me to either hide it or spend it on something they could never find.

Speaking of finding things, I've tucked in a few pictures of that actor you said you liked in the back of this book. He looks familiar but I can't place him. Strange to know that he's probably dead, either in pieces or shuffling around with the rest of the ticks. Or maybe there's an underground bunker somewhere, filled with anxious beautiful people who were once deemed important. Waiting on a miracle cure.

That's got to be it. Otherwise, why would the leeches want our blood?

As for nightmares, I used to have one as a teenager. I'd be walking on a beach, then I'd find a sandcastle and once I stepped in front of it, it grew huge, with a moat of foamy seawater and doors made of tiny shells. Inside, there were crabs wearing crowns and clicking their pincers at me. Maybe it sounds dumb, but it scared me for some reason. I swore off seafood for most of my teen life.

Stay alive,

A

A

Last time I was in Maryland, I was engaged to a gorgeous redhead who ended up spurning me for some moron who looked like a thumb. Here's hoping they didn't make it to the bunker where all the rich assholes wait for the leeches to bleed us dry.

They keep thinking they've got me, showing up after I've already left and tearing through everything, shouting my name and pleading for me to come out. Screaming about saving humanity, how we're the key to survival, our DNA and plasma is unlike anything they've seen, etc. Then they find my trail of breadcrumbs, and it's honestly hilarious watching them go up like kernels of popcorn. Pop, pop, pop, there goes your unremarkable DNA all over the other hazmat suits as they run in panicked circles, wanting to escape but not knowing where to run to. I usually cull most of them from the landmines alone, then the ticks usually show up to finish off the wounded and the ones who think they can hide. You'd think the leeches would have learned by now that the ticks pick up on all forms of motion. Terror can make people freeze up, but at some point, fight or flight kicks in and then they're running and, well. You know the rest.

It's funny, I used to think you were one of them, once I convinced myself you weren't just a figment of my imagination. I thought, "Maybe they got wise and they'll lure me out somewhere and they'll be waiting for me, drag me off to some lab to dissect me and study me like I'm a goddamned alien". But then I saw you take out a good number of ticks and leeches alike with that rifle, blasting 80s music with the boombox I left for you in New York. Damned shame that boombox didn't make it, but seeing a couple of jackasses, living and dead, eat a few bullets while listening to Culture Club was most certainly a highlight of my life.

Hope you're doing okay.

In my college days (before I dropped out), I would sometimes dream of living in a log cabin, hunting and fishing throughout the day, watching beavers build dams and listening to meadowlarks sing pretty little songs while I'd light a fire and stare at the night sky.

Keep breathing

— H

H,

I was nervous to see your last letter. All the way to Sky County, Oregon from the east coast is a hell of a trip. I used to want to drive cross country, just me and some friends, good music, wind in our hair, doing whatever the hell we wanted. Never got around to it, which is a damned shame, but in the greater scheme of things, I suppose it's irrelevant.

To be honest, I thought you were one of them too, for the same reasons. What were the chances someone else had the same genetic Get Out of Jail Free card? My relatives weren't so lucky, or unlucky, depending on how you see it. I've seen our charts, and we're not related, so your guess is as good as mine.

My realization came when I saw you nail boards on the building that contained the leeches that almost got a hold of me, in what was their headquarters in the middle of the desert. I watched you open a door to let a few ticks in, then you sat back and waited until it was clear from the screams within that the undead found their next meal. You shouted a few things at them I couldn't hear, flipped them off, then set the building on fire. Gotta tell you, I almost fell in love with you when I watched you laugh as they begged you for mercy.

*Did I ever tell you about the dream I had of a Christmas morning with tons of presents in gold and red, under a big tree and a twinkling star on top. I'd drink hot cocoa with the sweet bite of peppermint from a yellow mug and watch as my imaginary family tore into the presents with unbridled joy.*

*Stay alive,*

*A*



A



YOU'RE ALREADY ASLEEP, BUT I'M WRITING OUT OF HABIT. I'LL SHOW YOU THIS TOMORROW, MAYBE AFTER I USE ONE OF THE RATION PACKS TO MAKE COFFEE AND PANCAKES. THEY HAVE SOME SORT OF POWDERED CONCOCTION THAT CLAIMS TO BE "JUST LIKE EGGS", BUT I GUESS WE'LL SEE.

DAMN, BUT IT'S GOOD TO HAVE COMPANY.

I never saw this for myself, honestly. Thought I'd go through life alone, even before the dead started seeing the living as prey. When I broke out of the lab, I saw their charts and drawing boards, calling us Hope and Abundance, and I thought they were screwing with my head. They'd already taken a few pints at that point, so I was woozy, but I remember thinking that it just wasn't possible.

My next thought was, "We have to run".

I honestly don't remember finding your room, loosening the straps that had you confined to the hospital bed, or leading you to the nearest building, which was the newly renovated library, flush with supplies and plenty of places to hide. I can only remember waking up and finding your note, explaining how we could communicate by leaving letters in abandoned libraries, hiding details of our next destination in coded descriptions of dreams.

I don't know if they'll give up on finding us. Once people have something that gives them a reason to keep going, they grasp onto it until it's pried away. Maybe this shelter in the Great White North will keep us safe until we've become a myth, a fairy tale told by people who still somehow believe in a miracle.

One of them asked me once why I kept running. I'd found him, bleeding and bitten, and even though he knew not to bother asking for my help, he wanted to know why I didn't comply. When I told him it was because I didn't think we were worth saving, he asked about you. "What about your friend? You can't live in a world where it's just the two of you. At some point the dead will decay and there will be nothing left."

I told him, one person's hell is another's paradise, and how wonderful would it be to share paradise?

Besides, it's just like every generation does to the one before it. Talk a big game about leaving the world a better place than how you found it, but ultimately everyone pulls up the ladder so no one can follow.

But why pull up the ladder when you can smash it into splinters?

In the meantime, we'll both keep breathing and stay alive.

H

# #4LIFE

## Patrick Tumblety

### Part I

---

**Big Nick Energy @NColton17** ☐☐☐☐☐                         Jan 5

Mom called and said to skip practice and run home. Said there was a terrorist attack and I'm not safe. Everyone here keeps posting about Washington getting bombed and nothing about here. Who cares? #NotHereNoFear

Big Nick Energy @NColton17 ☐☐☐☐☐                                  Jan 5

Mom quarantined at market. Wanted to go get her and bring her home but she told me to stay here. Got games, food, weed, and no supervision, so I aint gonna argue. #staycation

---

Big Nick Energy @NColton17 ☐☐☐☐☐                                  Jan 17

Hi. Because what else am I supposed to do right now? #waitingforvaccines

---

Big Nick Energy @NColton17☐☐☐☐☐                                   Jan 17

None of my Flutter Circle Flapped in days. I didn't know any of them IRL, but I can't help but feel sad, you know?

---

Big Nick Energy @NColton17☐☐☐☐☐                                   Jan 18

Saw Claudia limping down the street. Last I saw her alive was History class last Tuesday. Half her cheek is missing and she's still the hottest girl in school. #AlexanderHigh4Life

Big Nick Energy @NColton17 ☐☐☐☐☐                               Jan 22

Almost smoked out of weed. Mom still quarantined at market so who cares about the smell? Need to ration. Dealer lives (lived?) downtown. They got it 1st. Probably dead or turned.

Big Nick Energy @NColton17☐☐☐☐☐                                Jan 22

Checked on food. Running low. Moms phone losing battery but says to hold tight and use up the cans. Water still running. Only dead walking on streets. I'm bored. Some console servers still running. Played 4v4 with some strangers. Takes over an hour to find players 4 a match :(

BenFM @Grim616 replying to Big Nick Energy @NColton17     Jan 22

Dude!? You go to AH? Frosh here. Thought I was the only one left! WYA? #AlexanderHigh4lLife

Big Nick Energy @NColton17 replying to BenFM @Grim616    Jan 22

LOL froshmeat. Not telling you where I am. Glad your alive though. Play Hotzone 4v4?

---

Nick C Still Here! @NColton17 ☐☐☐☐☐    Jan 22

Changed my name. Bout time I guess. Way past new years. Lol. #christmastreestillup

---

Nick C Still Here! @NColton17 ☐☐☐☐☐    Jan 22

Shit. Only two news channels reporting. Virus is spreading. No update on vaccines. Moms phone is dead but sure she's cool. #Whereisthecure?

---

BenFM @Grim616 replying to Nick C Still Here! @NColton17    Jan 22

> Dude, are you F'n kidding me? We might be the only ones in town left! WYA?

Nick C Still Here! @NColton17 replying to BenFM @Grim616     Jan 22

Nah, fam. I tell you where I am and you steeeeeel my sheeeeeet. #IveSeenThisMovie

BenFM @Grim616 replying to Nick C Still Here! @NColton17     Jan 22

Are you fr? This isn't a movie. We should stick together...

Nick C Still Here! @NColton17 replying to BenFM @Grim616     Jan 22

I got all I need here. Brains in DC will think of something. Just gotta hold tight. #justanotherday

BenFM @Grim616 replying to Nick C Still Here! @Ncolton17     Jan 22

Are you in denial? Washington was hit first. It's an attack. No one is coming!

Nick C Still Here! @NColton17 replying to BenFM @Grim616     Jan 22

I got the windows boarded up and the doors locked. Don't make a move until the cure comes.

#conspiraciesarefortheweak

#naturenotterrorism

#getalife

#getbit

#chill

#silenced

BenFM @Grim616 replying to Nick C Still Here! @Ncolton17    Jan 22

[User silenced] Click **HERE** to unblock the user and see their reply

---

BenFM @Grim616 replying to Nick C Still Here! @Ncolton17    Jan 22

[User silenced] Click **HERE** to unblock the user and see their reply

---

BenFM @Grim616 replying to Nick C Still Here! @Ncolton17    Jan 22

[User silenced] Click **HERE** to unblock the user and see their reply

---

BenFM @Grim616 replying to Nick C Still Here! @Ncolton17    Jan 22

[User silenced] Click **HERE** to unblock the user and see their reply

Nick C Still Here! @NColton17 ☐☐☐☐☐                Feb 2

Game servers still up but not enough players. #whereiseverybody? #isitreallythatbad?

---

Nick C Still Here! @NColton17 ☐☐☐☐☐                Feb 6

Miss mom. Hope she's okay. #boysandtheirmoms

---

Nick C B Hungry! @NColton17 ☐☐☐☐☐                 Feb 8

Food is going bad. Running out of cans. Going to take the back streets to supermarket. I'll bring mom a charger. Hope the toilet paper wasn't ransacked. #fasterthanthedead!

---

BenFM @Grim616 replying to Nick C B Hungry! @Ncolton17     Feb 8

[User silenced] Click HERE to unblock the user and see their reply

Nick C(an't Catch Me)! @NColton17 ☐☐☐☐ Feb 8

Saw Mom. I can't... I'll post later, fam.

---

BenFM @Grim616 replying to Nick C(an't Catch Me)! @NColton17 Feb 8

[User silenced] Click <u>HERE</u> to unblock the user and see their reply

---

BenFM @Grim616 replying to Nick C(an't Catch Me)! @NColton17 Feb 14

[User silenced] Click <u>HERE</u> to unblock the user and see their reply

---

BenFM @Grim616 replying to Nick C(an't Catch Me)! @NColton17 Feb 23

[User silenced] Click <u>HERE</u> to unblock the user and see their reply

Nick C @NColton17 ☐☐☐☐     May 3

Couldn't sleep last night. Mom's bday today. Thinking about going out to find her and put her out of her misery. Don't know if I can do it. Been trying to hold out hope. Even celebs stopped Fluttering. No more news. Radio is also static. #issomeonecoming?

---

Nick C @NColton17 ☐☐☐☐     May 4

Need more food. Supermarket run today. Going to take care of Mom if she's still there.

---

BenFM @Grim616 replying to Nick C @NColton17    ☐☐    May 4

[User silenced] Click **HERE** to unblock the user and see their reply

Nick C @NColton17 ☐☐☐☐     May 4

Not as many shamblers as I saw last time. Ones I ran into were looking thinner than me. Good but I think that means there is no one left to eat. Shit.

Saw mom... I'll post later. Not that anyone is listening.

---

BenFM @Grim616 replying to Nick C @NColton17     ☐☐     May 4

[User silenced] Click **HERE** to unblock the user and see their reply

---

Nick C @NColton17 ☐☐☐☐     May 5

I saw her standing in the bread isle. Decomposing. I... took care of her.

I can't help but think I could have saved her if I pulled her out of that place in time and brought her home. I was just doing what she told me.

#Imsorrymom

> BenFM @Grim616 replying to Nick C @NColton17          May 4
>
> [User silenced] Click <u>HERE</u> to unblock the user and see their reply

# Part II

> Big Nick Energy @NColton17 □□□□□          Jan 5
>
> Mom called and said to skip practice and run home. Said there was a terrorist attack and I'm not safe. Everyone here keeps posting about Washington getting bombed and nothing about here. Who cares? #NotHereNoFear

Big Nick Energy @NColton17 ☐☐☐☐☐                                      Jan 5

Mom quarantined at market. Wanted to go get her and bring her home but she told me to stay here. Got games, food weed, and no supervision, so I aint gonna argue. #staycation

Big Nick Energy @NColton17 ☐☐☐☐☐                                     Jan 17

Hi. Because what else am I supposed to do right now? #waitingforvaccines

Big Nick Energy @NColton17☐☐☐☐☐                                      Jan 17

None of my Flutter Circle Flapped in days. I didn't know any of them IRL, but I can't help but feel sad, you know?

Big Nick Energy @NColton17☐☐☐☐☐                    Jan 18

Saw Claudia limping down the street. Last I saw her alive was History class last Tuesday. Half her cheek is missing and she's still the hottest girl in school. #AlexanderHigh4Life

---

Big Nick Energy @NColton17 ☐☐☐☐☐                    Jan 22

Almost smoked out of weed. Mom still quarantined at market so who cares about the smell? Need to ration. Dealer lives (lived?) downtown. They got it 1st. Probably dead or turned.

---

Big Nick Energy @NColton17☐☐☐☐☐                    Jan 22

Checked on food. Running low. Moms phone losing battery but says to hold tight and use up the cans. Water still running. Only dead walking on streets. I'm bored. Some console servers still running. Played 4v4 with some strangers. Takes over an hour to find players 4 a match :(

BenFM @Grim616 replying to Big Nick Energy @NColton17        Jan 22

Dude!? You go to AH? Frosh here. Thought I was the only one left! WYA? #AlexanderHigh4lLife

---

Big Nick Energy @NColton17 replying to BenFM @Grim616        Jan 22

LOL froshmeat. Not telling you where I am. Glad your alive though. Play Hotzone 4v4?

---

Nick C Still Here! @NColton17 ☐☐☐☐☐        Jan 22

Changed my name. Bout time I guess. Way past new years. Lol. #christmas-treestillup

Nick C Still Here! @NColton17 ☐☐☐☐☐                    Jan 22

Shit. Only two news channels reporting. Virus is spreading. No update on vaccines. Moms phone is dead but sure she's cool. #Whereisthecure?

---

BenFM @Grim616 replying to Nick C Still Here! @NColton17    Jan 22

Dude, are you F'n kidding me? We might be the only ones in town left! WYA?

---

Nick C Still Here! @NColton17 replying to BenFM @Grim616    Jan 22

Nah, fam. I tell you where I am and you steeeeeel my sheeeeeet. #IveSeenThisMovie

---

BenFM @Grim616 replying to Nick C Still Here! @NColton17    Jan 22

Are you fr? This isn't a movie. We should stick together...

Nick C Still Here! @NColton17 replying to BenFM @Grim616     Jan 22

I got all I need here. Brains in DC will think of something. Just gotta hold tight. #justanotherday

BenFM @Grim616 replying to Nick C Still Here! @Ncolton17     Jan 22

Are you in denial? Washington was hit first. It's an attack. No one is coming!

Nick C Still Here! @NColton17 replying to BenFM @Grim616    Jan 22

I got the windows boarded up and the doors locked. Don't make a move until the cure comes.

#conspiraciesarefortheweak

#naturenotterrorism

#getalife

#getbit

#chill

#silenced

BenFM @Grim616 replying to Nick C Still Here! @Ncolton17    Jan 22

[User unsilenced] My brother is in the CIA. He's been hauled up a bunker all week. This is not going to go away. It's an all-out viral attack. We HAVE TO stick together. Please, bruh.

BenFM @Grim616 replying to Nick C Still Here! @Ncolton17    Jan 22

[User unsilenced] Please, this isn't going to blow over. We grouped up and going across town for survivors and bringing them back. We can use help, especially from someone your size. Please.

BenFM @Grim616 replying to Nick C Still Here! @Ncolton17    Jan 22

[User unsilenced] If you help, we can head to the market on Main where your mother is at. They are all alive but surrounded.

BenFM @Grim616 replying to Nick C Still Here! @Ncolton17     Jan 22

[User unsilenced] Did you silence my Flutters!? We are in the middle of a zombie outbreak!?

---

Nick C Still Here! @NColton17 ☐☐☐☐☐     Feb 2

Game servers still up but not enough players. #whereiseverybody? #isitreallythatbad?

---

Nick C Still Here! @NColton17 ☐☐☐☐☐     Feb 6

Miss mom. Hope she's okay. #boysandtheirmoms

---

Nick C B Hungry! @NColton17 ☐☐☐☐☐     Feb 8

Food is going bad. Running out of cans. Going to take the back streets to supermarket. I'll bring mom a charger. Hope the toilet paper wasn't ransacked. #fasterthanthedead!

BenFM @Grim616 replying to Nick C B Hungry! @Ncolton17     Feb 8

[User unsilenced] Nick, do NOT go outside. It's getting worse. Your Mom... I'm sorry but no one in the supermarket made it. I'm so sorry, Nick. If you get this, we are at the school. There are a ton of us surviving. Come to the school!

---

Nick C(an't Catch Me)! @NColton17 ▢▢▢▢     Feb 8

Saw Mom. I can't... I'll post later, fam.

---

BenFM @Grim616 replying to Nick C(an't Catch Me)! @NColton17 Feb 8

[User unsilenced] Oh, Nick, I'm so sorry, man. I'm here. WE are here. At the school.

BenFM @Grim616 replying to Nick C(an't Catch Me)! @NColton17 Feb 14

[User unsilenced] I'm going to keep posting until you unsilence me. Come to the school.

BenFM @Grim616 replying to Nick C(an't Catch Me)! @NColton17 Feb 23

[User unsilenced] Still here, Nick. I'm glad to see you have not blocked me yet, so I know these messages will go through if you choose to unsilence my account.

Nick C @NColton17 ☐☐☐☐                                       May 3

Couldn't sleep last night. Mom's bday today. Thinking about going out to find her and put her out of her misery. Don't know if I can do it. Been trying to hold out hope. Even celebs stopped Fluttering. No more news. Radio is also static. #issomeonecoming?

Nick C @NColton17 ▢▢▢▢                    May 4

Need more food. Supermarket run today. Going to take care of Mom if she's still there.

---

BenFM @Grim616 replying to Nick C @NColton17    ▢▢    May 4

[User unsilenced] Nick, don't! A lot has happened! DO NOT GO TO THE MARKET!

---

Nick C @NColton17 ▢▢▢▢                    May 4

Not as many shamblers as I saw last time. Ones I ran into were looking thinner than me. Good but I think that means there is no one left to eat. Shit.

Saw mom... I'll post later. Not that anyone is listening.

BenFM @Grim616 replying to Nick C @NColton17      ⬜⬜      May 4

[User unsilenced] PLEASE TELL ME YOU DIDNT KILL HER. PLEASE!

Nick C @NColton17 ⬜⬜⬜⬜      May 5

I saw her standing in the bread isle. Decomposing. I... took care of her.

I can't help but think I could have saved her if I pulled her out of that place in time and brought her home. I was just doing what she told me.

#Imsorrymom

BenFM @Grim616 replying to Nick C @NColton17      ⬜⬜      May 5

[User unsilenced] Oh, God, Nick. No. No. My brother made it home. He told me they found a cure Nick. A Cure.

BenFM @Grim616 replying to Nick C @NColton17     □□     May 5

[User unsilenced] jfc nick. There is a cure. Not just for us. For them. You could have saved her, Nick.

# Part III

Nick Colton @NColton17 □□□□     May 15

@Grim616 I hope you are doing okay. I'm hungry, and I'm scared, but most of all, I'm lonely. I unsilenced your tweets out of curiosity and now I'm sitting here with a knife to my wrists. I killed my mom. I killed her twice. I'm sorry I didn't listen. I'm sorry I shut you out, man...

Nick Colton @NColton17 ☐☐☐☐                                May 15

@Grim616 I got to ask a favor. I'm saving a print of my Flutter posts. If we make it, if the vaccine goes around and people get cured, show them how stupid I am. Show them what not to do. Tell them to be strong, and to reach out and help others like you do.

BenFM @Grim616 replying to Nick Colton @NColton17     ☐  May 15

I'm not going to do that, Nick. Are you there? Before you take your own life, I need to tell you why I won't do what you asked.

Nick Colton @NColton17 replying to BenFM @Grim616 ☐        May 15

Wth? I know I'm a D-bag, but at least give me that.

**BenFM @Grim616 replying to Nick Colton @NColton17** ☐ May 15

I looked up your address in the school directory. I'm about two minutes away from your house. The best thing you can do for everyone is keep going and help as many people as you can. Your coming with us, and we are going to take back our town.

**Nick Colton @NColton17 replying to BenFM @Grim616** ☐☐ May 15

...you would risk yourself for me? After all I did?

**BenFM @Grim616 replying to Nick Colton @NColton17** ☐ May 15

Nick, I will risk myself for you because of all that you can do moving forward.

**BenFM @Grim616 replying to Nick Colton @NColton17** ☐ May 15

Besides... #AlexanderHigh4Life

**Nick Colton @NColton17 replying to BenFM @Grim616** ☐☐       May 15

#AlexanderHigh4Life

I'll be ready to leave when you get here, froshmeat.

# WET PAPER OVER SHARP BONE

## Cat Voleur

B,

I hope this letter finds you well.

Do you remember when people used to say that? Do you remember when people used to write letters?

I can imagine you here, asking me how old I think you are. It was emails, right? When we were growing up? When we knew each other. You and I used to text — God, do you remember cell phones? We're back to beepers here, in the safe zone. And not everyone gets them, just the politicians and the doctors. I thought we grew up in the wrong decade for me to ever have a beeper that people were envious of. I thought I grew up in the wrong decade to ever miss my beeper.

Oh yeah. I'm a doctor or politician. Can you believe it? I practice medicine now.

Aside from the fact that my entire field of study is more fascinating now than it has ever been, it's also completely useless. Our vernacular is rapidly evolving, but it's constructed with simplicity in mind, made of survival shorthand and the occasional morbid joke. We needed medics a lot more than we needed someone to analyze communication phenomenons. But it is fascinating, isn't it? The English that I speak sounds so different from the kind my children are learning.

Hell, the English I'm writing sounds different than the English I speak day to day. This... this is more like how I talked before. Associative regression, maybe? I'm talking to you and so it's like I'm in the past again.

How I wish I could be.

I had a really good life. I know you're looking at me, on the ground, with my brains blown out, and my flesh rotted all over the bag that I mean to seal this letter in, and you're thinking about how stupid I was to leave. If you recognize me at all, to bother checking the bag. If you still remember me. If I make it. There are so many uncertainties right now.

But assuming I'm there, and that this letter has found you well, I want you to know I was happy. Not today. Not the last few weeks. But overall. You were right about the safe zone, and you weren't. It wasn't what I'd hoped it would be, but it wasn't as bad as you said. It's okay.

I got married. I have two of the most beautiful children you could ask for. It's easy to laugh about my credentials and how I shouldn't be doing procedures, and how they don't make the distinction between types of doctorates here, but the truth is that I got to help people. Whether I should be allowed or not, I got to help. I eased a lot of pain for those who were sick and dying and in my last moments, I know more than ever how important that is. I wish I had someone now to do that for me.

I am happy with my choices. I wasn't perfect. But overall, I feel like I did things that made my life worthwhile. So you can imagine my surprise that I'm using this one, thin, sliver of a chance I have to say goodbye to — fuck. I'm running out of space.

Whatever you do, don't turn this paper over. I'll explain on the next sheet just don't... Don't. I need you to promise me you won't look at the back of this. I don't have time to scratch it out. You won't like what you see. Please. Don't.

**Hour 1: How Are You Feeling?**

> 56 minutes. That's how long it took from the time I got infected until they helicoptered me out of the outpost where I was stationed, and into the morgue with two of these damn log sheets. I radioed for help for 10 days. I narrated the people we lost. I counted the dead. But it only took 56 minutes once I pressed the damn infection button. But hey. They got me here just in time to fill out the damn paperwork of my death. I might be the first one to fill out all 24 hours. I feel fucking great about that.

**Hour 2: How Are You Feeling?**

> They seemed awfully excited about one of their own doctors getting infected. Makes you wonder if this wasn't their plan all along. They kept telling me to be as medically accurate as possible. I told them I'd need equipment for that. At least I think I did. I meant to. I might still have been in some shock on the ride over. I don't think it would have mattered. They've understood the science behind this for a long time. What they need is someone to describe how it feels. There's a little swelling starting around the infection site. But mostly I just feel sad.

**Hour 3: How Are You Feeling?**

> I still feel fine, relatively. Eating. Drinking. Temperature's normal. I've calmed down a bit. The bite is looking worse. The flesh isn't mottled yet, but the blood that's been exposed is black. It's getting thicker. Jellied. I have some questions for whoever designed this form. These little boxes are supposed to contain the rest of my life. It doesn't feel like enough space. I don't feel like I needed this same damned prompt every time. They don't ask about me. My life. If my delirium gets bad enough to the end that I need this question, asking won't make a difference.

**Hour 4: How Are You Feeling?**

> Right on time, I'm starting to feel achy. If I were smart, I'd fill out this whole damn sheet now, while I can still hold the pen. I'd just go by the books, by what we know is supposed to happen, and sign my damn name. It would be a strong argument against the dumbasses still in denial of what the virus does. My name would go down in history as the first person to complete the full log. My husband could claim the reward. I'd leave a legacy for my children. I wonder why no one has tried that. Or why they've failed. My issue is I care too damn much about the truth. Maybe that's why they chose me.

**Hour 5: How Are You Feeling?**

> At the end of the last hour I promised to stop feeling sorry for myself. Stop ranting. Focus up. Describe the symptoms. Save the rest of the space for important insights I might have... you know. Toward the end? Then the vomiting started at the top of this hour. It only lasted about seven minutes? Give or take. I was too weak after to check the time right away. It tasted like, in a word, death. Sick. Acrid. Sweet. It was chunky at first, and then I guess I ran out of solids. Soon it was black, watery bile. Or blood. I don't even know what my blood looks like now.

**Hour 6: How Are You Feeling?**

> I thought about filling this box out from the toilet. For a while I thought I wouldn't even be able to do that. Thought I couldn't crawl over to the table to get the damn forms without leaving a trail of shit behind me. You want the truth? Honest, unfiltered truth about this feels like? I feel like my fucking asshole has been torn open. I spent nearly forty minutes shitting my guts out, and I'm not 100% sure that's hyperbole. A lot of that I was also dry-heaving. My insides just wanted to come out I guess. It didn't much matter the exit.

**Hour 7: How Are You Feeling?**

> A little better, actually. Thanks for asking.
>
> There is a distinct possibility that I might actually have been able to doze off a little before the alarm reminded me to write.
>
> Compared to the last hour, I guess anything would feel like an improvement. But I really do feel better. No fever yet or anything.
>
> Scratch that, 103.

**Hour 8: How Are You Feeling?**

> Thirsty. I've never experienced thirst like this in my entire life. The water tastes bad — maybe it just tastes like water and my mouth tastes bad. But I'm chugging it down. There's plenty of it left for me, I guess they knew this would be a side effect. There's a lot of food too, but I can't imagine I'll ever feel like eating anything ever again. It's hard just to keep the water down, honestly, and I wasn't even managing that at the start of the hour. It tasted so bad.

**Hour 9: How Are You Feeling?**

> My stomach has settled a little. I'm still thirsty though. I'm shaking less than I have been, and can hold the pen with one hand. My left hand is steady enough I can hold the bottle while I write. I've splashed a little water on myself, and I'm still damp. Sweaty. I don't know if that was a side-effect of the fever or the vomiting or the diarrhea, or if the virus just makes me sweat. Doesn't matter. I'm going to take one last shower, while I'm still feeling up to it. One last, really human moment before it all goes down.

**Hour 10: How Are You Feeling?**

> Bad. The pressure in my head. Behind my eyes. White lights.
>
> I know my heart still beats. Can feel it. In. My. Brain.

**Hour 11: How Are You Feeling?**

> Throwing up again. Shorter bouts of vomiting. Looks/smells like a swamp in the toilet.
>
> Never dried off from the shower. Not sure if I'm sweating again? Still? Not sure if there are early signs of decay this fast. I didn't think that happened till the halfway point. Until I die? My skin is spongy. I've lost a lot of color. Maybe it just feels that way because I know it's coming. Maybe I'll be the first to log all 24 hours AND the first to discover a new, faster acting strain. Wouldn't that be something? Are these the kind of details you want? I don't know.

**Hour 12: How Are You Feeling?**

> I'm actually feeling really well. I'm not going to say I'm okay with what happened. But I never thought I'd feel this good again in the very short amount of time I have left. The last few hours have made me really appreciate the small things. That sick taste in my mouth isn't as strong. My muscles don't feel as weak. I'm thinking clearer. It feels like I could recover from this, even though I know I won't. And to tell you the truth, I'm just glad I get to help people by filling this out. I want there to be a record. I want everyone to have incentive to avoid this.

So, anyway.

Where was I?

I have this one chance to say goodbye and I'm not writing to my husband or our children. That was who I meant to write. And when I took the pen, I was thinking about you. I could only think about you

It will be easy, I hope, for them to remember me how I was. And better that they do. But you and I... we have unfinished business. And now it's never going to be finished. And for some reason I just can't stop thinking about that.

I'm not saying that I would go back. I wouldn't risk the good I've done or the life I've had or the lives of my kids. I love my kids more than anything. They're worth the rest of it. I wouldn't go back, even if I could. Even knowing I'm alone when I pass. Even knowing what I turn into. They're worth it. But I just can't stop thinking about how we left things.

You were—are—my one regret. I wanted to write and tell you that you were wrong not to come with me, but you would have hated it here. The rules. The regulations. The conspiracies. People want so badly for things to be the way they were that they won't work together to make a new normal that's worth having. So we're stuck at the same impasse. You were wrong not to come, and I believe that. But I also believe you would believe that you were right, if you could see it here.

I hope you're living your best life out there in the wilderness. I don't want you to read this and think about which one of us was wrong, or suffered more for it. I'd never hope for you to feel the weight of these questions as I do. I just want you to know, I guess, that in the end, I was thinking about you.

I hope you didn't turn the paper over. I don't want you to read the log of what I'm going through. That's what's on the back of these pages and it's honest. It's angry. It's an unbearable kind of sad.

You're going to think that this is really twisted, but when someone gets infected, they're asked to document their symptoms. No one has ever been coherent through all twenty-four hours between the bite and when the heart stops. It sounds like an awful thing to take pride in... but I could have been the first one on record. I would have been proud in my last moments, if I didn't need that paper to write this.

I threw away my chance at glory so I could say one last goodbye. And after all these years, you were the person I missed the most.

I don't want you to worry. I'm in the last hour now, and it doesn't hurt. I won't feel the metal as it pierces these pages to my flesh. I'll try to anchor it deep in the bone so it stays on the journey. I don't know what will happen once I leave this place, but you're on my mind. You're the last thing that will ever be on my mind, and I hope my body knows to follow that thought back home to you.

Even after all this time.

I don't care how this letter finds you. I just hope that it does. I hope you're the one standing above me when I fall.

- L

**Hour 13: How Are You Feeling?**

> I'm not going to lie, there's some pain. I'm feeling better overall, energy-wise. My mental faculties are... better. Better than they were. Maybe not in Hour 12, but in most of the hours before that. What scares me most is that I should be getting tired. But I'm not. My heart is beating too fast. I thought it was supposed to be slowing down at this point, but it feels like it's just trying to beat its way out of my chest cavity from the inside. Can it do that? My skin feels so soft. Like wet paper over sharp bones.

**Hour 14: How Are You Feeling?**

> Hungry. Now I am grateful that they left me with food. It isn't raw meat, like they say that you crave toward the end. Do they say that? I feel like they do, but I'm having a tough time remembering what order the symptoms are supposed to come in. It's as hungry as I've ever been, and I'm glad that they left me with food. It's mush, mostly, MREs, but they taste better than anything I can ever remember eating. Is that the virus? Is that a real symptom of the virus that it impacts my taste? Or is that just a side effect of being so damn hungry?

**Hour 15: How Are You Feeling?**

> Honestly, I feel okay. 15 hours in, and aside from still eating nonstop, I feel great. The food is giving me strength. I haven't slept in... well, a long time, but I'm feeling stronger and more energized than I have been since even before I was bitten. I feel so good that part of me wonders if there wasn't a mistake. There are rumors that some people might be immune? Or, maybe this is a new strain. I know how that sounds. How futile. How silly. But I don't feel like a dying woman right now. I don't feel like it's possible I'm less than ten hours away from death.

**Hour 16: How Are You Feeling?**

> The change is starting. I'm still hungry. Getting hungrier by the minute. But the food tastes awful in my mouth. My stomach is rumbling when I'm not shoving something down my gullet, but all the sustenance feels wrong. It tastes wrong. Like nothing. Like static. Like ash. It is bone dry and I can barely choke down enough to make a difference in my stomach. I'll be the first to say it too... the energy is here. My mental faculties are here. But I'm not looking so great. The bags under my eyes are worse. I don't have a lot of color left. The black in my veins is spreading.

**Hour 17: How Are You Feeling?**

> It's getting easier to choke the food down. I find my jaw working constantly, even when I'm not putting more food in my mouth. It's chewing constantly, without me. My teeth clack together when there's not jerky or crackers or that damn, cold soup between them to slow them down. Clack. Clack. Clack. Each damn clack is like a fucking nail being hammered into my brain. The migraine is back with a vengeance. The hunger is worse. And that damned ashy taste has settled in. Like it's normal. I guess this is my new normal.

**Hour 18: How Are You Feeling?**

> Here they are. The cravings. The meat. Do you remember when we used to go to steakhouses? When that was a thing? Chain restaurants... steak houses. I was all a medium gal, but you, you were... wait. Who is this to? Fuck, the papers. Right, right. It doesn't matter. We all eat all our meat well done now, for fear of the contamination. And I want meat. Not the jerky they stocked for me. Fresh meat. Raw meat. I guess that is a thing they say. Not a rumor or a myth or a hokey cliché. The cravings are real. They're a part of it.

**Hour 19: How Are You Feeling?**

> Not so hungry anymore. Now I just hurt. I don't know if it's because I ate so much. I don't know if it's because I'm changing. I feel all twisted up. I could be imagining it, but when I look in the mirror I see myself as green. Cartoon, fucking seasick green. Do you remember cartoons? I'd be scared of puking up my guts again, but I don't think they're mine anymore. I don't know how to describe this, but even through the pain, they feel detached? Decaying? They're not a part of me. This pain isn't from me. All my insides are twisted up into something else.

**Hour 20: How Are You Feeling?**

> It doesn't hurt anymore. Is that a good thing, or a bad thing? I'm starting to get a little tired, it's been a day — almost a full day, but I absolutely feel strong enough to make it to the end. Is it wrong that I'm almost disappointed? 5 more hours of this, counting this hour, and that will be it. There was no big finish, no big revelation. I'm just here, alone, doing my duty, filling out the paperwork, these tiny little boxes. I almost wish there had been an intervention. That I wasn't the first to make it. If I weren't so damn close to being the first person ever... It doesn't matter.

**Hour 21: How Are You Feeling?**

> The cold came on very quickly. I have the thermostat all the way up. I have all the blankets. All the coats. I wonder if the last people who wore these were infected too? Not that it matters. Sterilization, security measures, they don't mean shit when you're dying. They have me locked in tightly, from the side of the safe zone. I'll never get back into that side. Never see my husband, my children. What's left of my colleagues. If I didn't think I'd make the 24 hours, I'd write them, instead of finishing. I'd take the back of these sheets and I would say goodbye.

**Hour 22: How Are You Feeling?**

> They didn't answer me, when I asked for help. When I asked for paper. For heat. I can feel the deterioration begin. It's really set in now. I'm right on schedule, but I'm already so tired. I can't believe I have three more hours of this, counting this coming hour. I can make it, right? Right? I'd make a run for it, just run through the side of the facility that isn't locked, but I'm so close. I'm two hours away, and I'm right on schedule. I don't know who I'd write anyway... my husband, right? He'd have an easier time breaking the contents of the news... right?

**Hour 23: How Are You Feeling?**

> I'm not going to make it.
>
> What the fuck am I doing? I need to say goodbye.

**Hour 24: How Are You Feeling?**

# Contributors

## Angel Krause

Angel Krause runs the horror YouTube channel Voices from the Mausoleum. She had a short published for the first time in 2022 and works closely with the horror indie writing community to promote and create new stories. Projects include a horror series called 'That Old House', an anthology series that focuses each installment to just one room of the house. She works with multiple charity anthologies including one for reproductive rights and more recently a wolf conservation charity anthology about werewolves! You can find her on all social media platforms.

## Tom Coombe

Tom Coombe is a Pennsylvania-based horror writer whose stories have appeared in a number of web publications and print anthologies. You can find him at CalmTomb on both Twitter and BlueSky, mostly the latter.

# Casey Masterson

Casey Masterson (she/her/hers) is a horror author with publications in Dark Matter Magazine. Shortwave Publishing, and Poe Boy Publishing. Her debut collection of short stories, *Revelations of the Raven Master*, was published August 31, 2023. When she is not writing, Casey enjoys reading and playing with her animals. You can find Casey on various socials here;  IG mastersonc27, Twitter: kaseejedimaster, Blue Sky: kasseejedimaster.bsky.social

# Sophie Ingley

Sophie Ingley writes horror and scribbles spooky stuff. She's also a music geek and movie nerd. Three of her favourite things are coffee, the smell of books, and the sound of rain against her window on a day off. Follow her online. It could be fun.
@SophieIngley Twitter
sophieingley Instagram

## Samantha Arthurs

Samantha Arthurs is a horror author and Appalachian poet. Her published works include the Rag & Bone trilogy, the Dreadful Seasons series, and a plethora of horror shorts and poems. When she isn't writing she enjoys reading and reviewing books, hanging out with her dogs, recording her podcast (The Appalachian Spooky Hour), and watching horror movies. She was born and raised in Appalachia, and still happily resides there.

## Maria Hossain

Maria Hossain is a writer based in Dhaka, Bangladesh. Their short fiction has appeared in Translunar Traveler's Lounge magazine.

## Andrew Harrowell

Andrew is a multi-genre writer, with three self-published books (a light-hearted present day take on mythology, a dystopian whodunit, and a coming-of-a-very-young-age tale about the anxiety of going to nursery), plus a horror novella released with an independent publisher. He was also one of ten authors selected for inclusion in horror anthology The Hyperion: Tales from Hell. You can find out a bit more about him on X and Threads: @HarrowellAndrew.

# S. C. Fisher

S. C. Fisher is the author of horror series Base Fear, as well as short story contributions that have featured in anthologies such as That Old House: The Bathroom, Sinister Stories by the Ten, and Horrorscope Volume 4. She lives in Britain with her husband, their children, and more animals than she can count on one hand.

# Emma Jamieson

Growing up in a haunted house in a forest which was an infamous spot for burning those accused of witchcraft, all things morbid, spooky and dark were in Emma's destiny. She has always found comfort and beauty in things others may find terrifying and frequently seek solitude in graveyards. Embracing her creative streak, Emma has performed in the Edinburgh Festival Fringe and has several short stories published within various horror anthologies. She is an enormous horror movie geek, has an abnormal fascination with serial killers and can be found sharing her bookish ramblings on Instagram @book_nooks_spooks

# T.T. Madden

T.T. Madden (they/them) is a genderfluid, mixed-race writer whose work has appeared most recently in Shadows Over Main Street Vol. 3 and Dead Letters: Episodes of Epistolary Horror. They have two novellas coming out in 2024, The Cosmic Color, with Neon Hemlock, and The Familialists, with Off Limits Press. They can be found on Twitter, Bluesky, TikTok, and Instagram @ttmaddenwrites.

# Andy Rau

Andy lives in west Michigan with his wife and two children, all of whom share an interest in horror stories and games. He is co-host of the Roll for Topic tabletop gaming podcast, where zombies, Cthulhu, and other supernatural menaces are a regular topic of conversation. You can keep up with the podcast and Andy's other projects at www.stagingpoint.com.

# Madeline White

Madeline lives on a large farm in rural NY with her partner. By day she makes wool art and takes care of her livestock, by night she writes grimdark fiction as a break from her cottagecore Reality. You can find her on IG @light_in_the_grimdark

# Christina Wilder

Christina Wilder was born in Santiago, Chile, and grew up in New Jersey and Florida. Her writing has been featured in Coffin Bell and short story anthologies including What One Wouldn't Do and Dead Letters. She lives in Tacoma, WA with her husband Chris and cat Bella. Besides writing, she is also an actor and has done voice acting for the Decoded Horror Channel. She can be found on Instagram @christinamwilder.

# Patrick Tumblety

Patrick Tumblety is an author of horror, science-fiction, and poetry. He has been featured in numerous anthologies, including Tales of Jack the Ripper from **Word Horde Press**, The Dead Inside, from **Dark Dispatch,** Gothic Fantasy: Science Fiction, from **Flame Tree Publishing**, and Dark Moon Digest from **Perpetual Motion Machine Publishing**. He has also been published by and is an active member of the **Horror Writers Association**. His work has been described as being able to deliver both "genuine fear and genuine hope." (Amy H. Sturgis - Award-Winning Author and Professor of Narrative Studies)

# Cat Voleur

Cat Voleur is the author of Revenge Arc, and a proud mother to all the rescue felines. You can find her co-hosting Slasher Radio, and The Nic F'n Woo Cage Cast. When she's not creating or consuming morbid content you can find her pursuing her passion for fictional languages.

VOICES

FROM THE MAUSOLEUM

PUBLISHING

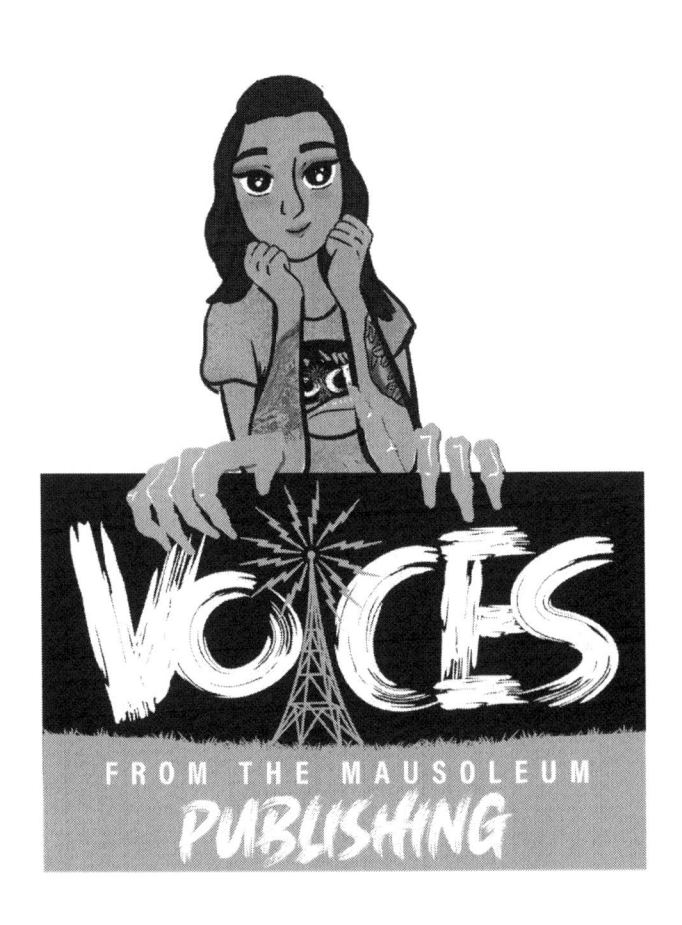

Cover design services for the beautifully creepy. Premades, customs, magazine covers, etc.

Twitter: @grimpoppydesign

Patreon: patreon.com/grimpoppydesign